j
K

10,202

Keene, Carolyn
By the light of the study lamp

BY THE LIGHT OF
THE STUDY LAMP

Books by

CAROLYN KEENE

Nancy Drew Mystery Stories

The Secret of the Old Clock
The Hidden Staircase
The Bungalow Mystery
The Mystery at Lilac Inn
The Secret at Shadow Ranch
The Secret of Red Gate Farm
The Clue in the Diary
Nancy's Mysterious Letter
The Sign of the Twisted Candles
The Password to Larkspur Lane
The Clue of the Broken Locket
The Message in the Hollow Oak
The Mystery of the Ivory Charm
The Whispering Statue
The Haunted Bridge
The Clue of the Tapping Heels
The Mystery of the Brass Bound
Trunk
The Mystery at the Moss-Covered
Mansion
The Quest of the Missing Map

The Clue in the Jewel Box
The Secret in the Old Attic
The Clue in the Crumbling Wall
The Mystery of the Tolling Bell
The Clue in the Old Album
The Ghost of Blackwood Hall
The Clue of the Leaning Chimney
The Secret of the Wooden Lady
The Clue of the Black Keys
The Mystery at the Ski Jump
The Clue of the Velvet Mask
The Ringmaster's Secret
The Scarlet Slipper Mystery
The Witch Tree Symbol
The Hidden Window Mystery
The Haunted Showboat
The Secret of the Golden
Pavilion
The Clue in the Old Stagecoach
The Mystery of the Fire Dragon
The Clue of the Dancing Puppet

The Moonstone Castle Mystery

Dana Girls Mystery Stories

By the Light of the Study Lamp
The Secret at Lone Tree Cottage
In the Shadow of the Tower
A Three-Cornered Mystery
The Secret at the Hermitage
The Circle of Footprints
The Mystery of the Locked Room
The Clue in the Cobweb
The Secret at the Gatehouse
The Mysterious Fireplace
The Clue of the Rusty Key
The Portrait in the Sand

The Secret in the Old Well
The Clue in the Ivy
The Secret of the Jade Ring
Mystery at the Crossroads
The Ghost in the Gallery
The Clue of the Black Flower
The Winking Ruby Mystery
The Secret of the Swiss Chalet
The Haunted Lagoon
The Mystery of the Bamboo Bird
The Sierra Gold Mystery
The Secret of Lost Lake

Suddenly through the bare branches Louise saw the face
of Jake Garbone

BY THE LIGHT
OF THE
STUDY LAMP

By

CAROLYN KEENE

Grosset & Dunlap, *Publishers*

NEW YORK

CONTENTS

viii   Contents

CHAPTER I

UNCLE NED'S GIFT

"OH, LOUISE, you haven't read Uncle Ned's letter yet! Do stop a minute and listen!"

Louise Dana, a pretty, dark-haired girl of seventeen, paused in the doorway with an armful of paper novelties. The glow of the library lamp shone upon the fair hair and eager face of her sister, Jean, who was curled up in an easy chair with the letter in her hand.

"Please!" begged Jean. "You can sort those novelties for the party later. Come over and listen to the letter."

"I have a hundred and one things to do, getting things ready for the guests," said Louise as she dumped the favors on the table, "but after all we don't hear from Uncle Ned every day in the week. What has the old darling to say for himself?"

"He's sending us a present!"

1

"A present!" exclaimed Louise, perching herself on the arm of the chair. "That's exciting. The old dear is always planning some sort of surprise for us. What is it? When will it be here?"

"Patience, sister! Patience!" laughed Jean. "If you'll just calm yourself for a few minutes I'll read you the letter."

"When will Uncle Ned be home?"

"Tomorrow. The *Balaska* docked at New York yesterday. Wait—it's all here in the letter." Jean glanced up with a smile.

" 'My Dear Nieces: Just a few lines to let you know that I am back in the U. S. A. again, the *Balaska* having docked safely a few hours ago. We had rough weather from Cherbourg out, but the last two days of the voyage were fine. I shall be back in Oak Falls the day after you receive this letter and hope I find you well and ready for school again. We shall miss you around the house, but of course your Aunt Harriet will feel your absence most keenly. An old sea captain like myself, away from home for weeks at a time, can scarcely find a chance to get acquainted with his women folk'——"

Jean giggled.

"Women folk! I feel quite grown-up."

"——'but that is my loss more than yours. I picked up a little gift for you in New York today and it is being sent on to you by express. It is an antique lamp and the dealer said it was more valuable than it looks. Hoping you like the present and looking forward to seeing you soon, I remain, Your loving Uncle Ned.' "

The girls were pleased and excited.

"A lamp!" exclaimed Louise. "Isn't that lovely of him. Why, it's just what we need for our study room at Starhurst!"

"An *antique!* We'll be the envy of the school, having an antique lamp in our study."

Jean and Louise were planning an early return to the Starhurst School for Girls in the near-by town of Penfield, where the coming semester would see them in their sophomore year. The girls were orphans and they lived in the rambling country house of their Uncle Ned Dana, on the outskirts of Oak Falls. As the letter indicated, they saw very little of their bluff, elderly relative, whose duties as captain of the great Atlantic liner *Balaska* kept him away from home for weeks at a time. The house was in charge of Aunt Harriet, who was Captain Ned's sister, a good-natured, attractive maiden lady in her middle forties. The presence of two lively young girls in the house, the clumsy diligence of Ben Harrow, the stuttering hired man, and the aggravating stupidity of Cora Appel, the maid, kept life interesting for Aunt Harriet.

"He said it would be sent by express," said Jean, glancing at the letter again. "I can hardly wait to see it."

A clamorous knock at the back door sent the sisters scurrying wildly out of the room.

"The expressman!" exclaimed Louise. "I'm sure it can't be anyone else."

The newcomer proved to be the expressman. He stood there at the back door with a heavy box under his arm.

"I hope you haven't banged it around," said Jean breathlessly.

"No, Miss," he assured her, grinning. "There's so many signs on it sayin' 'Fragile' and 'Handle with Care' that I've been wonderin' if it holds dynamite."

He set the box down carefully on the kitchen floor and took his receipt book from his pocket. Louise signed the slip while Jean rummaged through the tool chest in the cupboard for chisel and hammer.

When the expressman went away, whistling cheerily, they carefully opened the box. There was a tremendous amount of excelsior and packing, so that it was some time before Uncle Ned's gift was finally revealed. Jean, boyish and gay, was dancing with excitement as her sister removed the last layer of newspaper from around the lamp.

"Why, it's gorgeous!" she gasped, as Louise held up the beautiful ornament.

"I never saw anything so lovely!" exclaimed Louise.

It was, in truth, an exquisite lamp of graceful

design and intricate workmanship. When Jean had further explored the box and had located the shade, she held it above the lamp standard, so that they realized the complete beauty of the gift. They could well believe that it was a valuable antique, for it had an appearance of age and solidity. It was not old-fashioned, for the artistry of its design was of the sort that belongs to all time. It had been cunningly modernized by the addition of wiring that fitted it for electricity.

"Dear Uncle Ned!" said Louise softly. "He couldn't have given us a more beautiful present."

"I wonder how old it is. Did you ever see such a lovely design as the one on the base——"

At that moment there was a startling interruption.

Crash!

The sound came from the upper part of the house. The loud noise was followed by the tinkle of shattered glass and then by an ear-splitting scream.

"What on earth—!" exclaimed Louise.

Jean was already speeding toward the door.

"It's Applecore! Perhaps she's fallen out of a window."

Louise hastily set down the lamp on the kitchen table and hurried after her sister.

"Applecore" was Jean's characteristic nick

name for buxom, red-cheeked Cora Appel, the
maid. The best that could be said for Cora was
that she was willing to learn. She was, unfortunately, a clumsy and heavy-handed girl,
and it was a dull day in the Dana household if
Cora did not manage to fall down the cellar
stairway or smash a few plates or otherwise
disastrously inform the household that her education was proceeding apace. However, in all
the history of the young lady's service in the
Dana home, her activities had never produced
such a terrific crash, such a blood-curdling
scream as that which now startled the girls.

They hurried madly up the stairs. From a
room above they could hear Applecore wailing
and sobbing.

"What *has* happened?" gasped Louise.

"She's still alive, anyway. I can hear her
bawling."

Jean raced down the upper hall, with Louise
at her heels. The girls dashed into the room
from which emanated the heart-rending sobs,
and there they found the wretched Cora. She
was sitting on the floor, completely surrounded
by broken glass, with the shattered frame of a
wall mirror at her feet.

"Get a doctor!" wailed the frightened maid.
"I'm all cut to bits. I'm hurt bad. I think I
broke an artery or somethin'—oh, oh—and
when I was bein' so careful with that
mirror——"

She raised her nose in the air and began to howl.

Louise made a quick survey of the damage. The mirror was shattered beyond repair, but she was more concerned with Cora's injuries. Upon examination it was found, however, that the girl had sustained only a few slight cuts from the flying glass.

"I'll get some bandages and salve," said Louise, and flew from the room.

"Never mind the bandages," wept Cora, a forlorn picture as she sat on the floor among the fragments of the mirror. "I don't want 'em."

"But you've been cut by the glass," protested Jean as she knelt beside the maid.

"I don't care," Cora sniffled. "I want this awful mess cleared up before Miss Harriet comes back. Oh, what she will say to me, I dunno."

"Never mind. Never mind, Applecore," soothed Jean. "She won't scold you. It was an accident, I'm sure."

"Of course it was an accident," wept Cora. "You don't think I go around upsettin' lookin'-glasses on purpose, do you? I never done such a turrible thing in my whole life before. I'm so sorry I don't know what to do."

"Never mind. I think it was not a very valuable mirror anyway. As long as you're not badly hurt, it doesn't matter."

Cora's eyes were round with amazement.

"Doesn't matter, Miss Jean!" And then she began to sob again. "Oh, dear me, I break a big mirror and she says it doesn't matter. Seven years' bad luck it means, and she says it doesn't matter. Oh, dear, how will I ever get through the next seven years?"

She sat there, sniffling and dabbing at her eyes with the corner of her apron. Jean wanted to laugh, but at that moment her sister hurried into the room with the bandages and salve. Louise, who was older than Jean, was the more serious of the two and the more efficient in an emergency.

"Now," she said in a businesslike manner, "hold out your arm, Cora, and we'll dress those cuts. They aren't very bad, but they need some attention——"

"Never mind me," wailed Cora. "I want all this busted glass out of the way before Miss Harriet comes back. She'll think I'm the clumsiest girl on the face of the earth."

"Don't worry about Aunt Harriet. I'll clear away the wreckage," promised Jean. "While Louise is on hospital duty, I'll get the broom and dustpan."

Jean danced out of the room and skipped lightly down the stairs. Applecore's concern for the removal of the broken glass appealed to her as laughable, for the maid had no reason to fear the return of Aunt Harriet. That lady was the soul of kindness, and whatever her per-

sonal feelings might be about the destruction
of the mirror, she would never scold the maid
for what was obviously an accident. This Jean
knew.

The younger Dana girl went out into the
kitchen and took the broom and dustpan from
the closet in which they were kept. As she
passed the box in which Uncle Ned's present
had arrived, she glanced at the table and then
paused in surprise.

The precious study lamp was not there!

Jean was startled. She distinctly remembered seeing Louise set the lamp on the table
when Applecore's scream rang through the
house. Not five minutes had passed since then.
She ran to the foot of the stairs and called to
her sister.

"Louise! Did you move the lamp?"

"The lamp?" Louise called back in surprise.
"Why, no."

"Then where is it?"

"Right on the kitchen table where I left it."

"But it isn't, Louise!" cried Jean. "The
lamp is gone. My goodness, it must have been
stolen."

"Stolen?"

There was a triumphant wail from Cora
Appel.

"Didn't I tell you? Seven years' bad luck
for this house and it's startin' already."

CHAPTER II

The Secondhand Shop

Louise was downstairs in a moment. The girls ran back into the kitchen. There was the box, there was the packing—but the lamp was gone.

"How could it have disappeared in that time!" exclaimed Louise in bewilderment. "Someone must have walked in here the moment we went upstairs."

Suddenly they noticed a sound from the road at the side of the house.

"Listen!" said Jean.

They heard the roar of a motor as if a car was just being driven away.

Louise fled madly through the house, flung open the front door, and ran out onto the veranda. She was just in time to see a car vanishing out of the driveway into the main road that passed in front of the Dana home.

Louise was a quick-thinking girl and her first idea was to get the license number of the car. The end of the driveway was only about thirty yards away, so she was able to see the license plate distinctly. The number was firmly imprinted on her mind before the automobile had swung out into the road and disappeared beyond the trees.

Louise turned to find Jean at her side.

"There goes our lamp!" she said grimly.

"And we're going after it," decided Jean. "Come on, Lou! We'll follow that car."

Jean snatched their coats from a closet and the girls rushed around to the garage at the back of the house, where the family roadster was parked. Hastily they scrambled into it. Louise stepped on the starter, backed the light car into the driveway, swung it around, and then sped toward the main road.

"I took the license number," she told Jean. "It's B7953. Even if we don't catch him now, we'll find out who owns that car, anyway."

Once on the highway she stepped on the accelerator and the roadster leaped forward. Jean's blonde bobbed hair streamed wildly in the wind and she put her hands over it to hold it down firmly. There was no sign of the other car on the road ahead, but it was a winding highway and the fugitive had several minutes' start.

"What on earth," exclaimed Jean, "could possess anyone to steal our lamp? The thief must have known about it. Unless he was a tramp——"

"Tramps don't travel around in automobiles," Louise pointed out logically as she bore down on the wheel at a sharp curve. "No, it was planned. The man must have followed the express driver and then watched his chance."

"Why, he may have been looking through the window all the time we were unpacking the lamp!" said Jean. "But I still can't understand why he would want to steal it."

"Uncle Ned said it was an antique, and valuable," said Louise. "Perhaps it's even more valuable than he thought."

"We scarcely had time to look at it," said Jean disconsolately. "Oh, I do hope we get it back. Did you notice how many people were in the car?"

"Just one man, as far as I could see."

Louise bent forward over the wheel, her eyes fixed on the ribbon of highway ahead. They were approaching the outskirts of Oak Falls. As the roadster sped around a curve, the town came into view, its spires and rooftops rising above the trees along the banks of the river. Then Jean uttered a cry of delight:

"There's the car! We're catching up to him, Louise!"

About a quarter of a mile ahead the other car was racing toward the town at headlong speed. Louise let the roadster out as much as she dared. It rocked and swayed as it ate up the highway in pursuit.

The fugitive was a good driver, his car was

powerful, and it was evident that he realized he was being chased. He defied all the speed laws as he sped across the big bridge over the Oak River.

Louise groaned.

"He'll be into the traffic before we can over-take him."

This, obviously, was the man's objective. Oak Falls was a busy community, and one of its heaviest traffic arteries was the street lead-ing toward the bridge. Just before the girls reached the river a small automobile swung out of a side road and approached the bridge at a leisurely speed, while at the same time a heavy truck came rumbling out onto the bridge. Louise could not cut in ahead of the other car. She was forced to slow down. Exasperated, the sisters saw the car ahead vanish into the traffic beyond the bridge.

As the truck rumbled by, Louise swung the roadster out and raced ahead of the little car that had held them up. Out on the street be-yond the bridge she sped along until they were forced to halt at a stop-light. Away ahead they thought they could see the top of the other car, but they could not be sure, as the traffic was heavier now, being fed by a constant stream of cars and trucks from the side streets. By the time the go-light shone they realized that they had lost the fugitive.

"What dreadful luck!" exclaimed Jean.

"We'll have no chance of finding him now."

Louise was thoughtful. Her pretty face became serious.

"I don't know about that. If he followed the expressman out to our place, he must have come from Oak Falls. It's hardly likely that he'll go on to some other town. We may run across that car yet."

"Then we'll search every street in Oak Falls," declared Jean with determination.

They drove on, more slowly now because of the traffic, into the business section of the town. The two girls kept a sharp lookout for all parked cars and studied every license plate, but there was no sign of the mysterious "B7953."

They drove back and forth for some time without result, then pulled up to the curb.

"Let's leave the roadster here," suggested Louise finally, "and walk around. I'll take the streets on one side of the downtown section. You take the others. Perhaps we'll find the man's car parked somewhere."

"Good idea," Jean agreed, as they clambered out. Jean suggested that they notify the police station, but Louise would not hear of it.

"I like mysteries," she declared, "and this is something of a mystery. We'll handle it ourselves. If I find the man who drove that car, I'll give him a piece of my mind."

The girls separated to follow out their plan

of searching the side streets. Jean was glowing with excitement as she left the busy main thoroughfare and plunged down an ugly, narrow street of cheap stores and warehouses. It was the first unusual adventure the girls had experienced during their vacation, and she was enjoying it to the utmost.

She was puzzled as to the motive for the theft of the study lamp. It was an antique, of course, and Uncle Ned had said it was valuable, yet she knew he was not rich enough to afford a very expensive gift. It had evidently tempted the robber to take extraordinary risks.

"I can't understand why he should come in broad daylight and steal it from right under our noses," she said to herself. "He might have waited until night."

She came out onto a gloomy little street, squalid and wretched in the light of the cloudy October afternoon. There was but one car parked by the curb and as she walked quickly down the sidewalk it seemed to her that the machine was familiar. Jean looked at the dirty license plate.

Then she gasped. It was the car she sought. There was the number—B7953, and unless Louise had made a serious mistake, it was the same car that had sped away from the Dana home not half an hour previously. The automobile was unoccupied.

Jean examined the building before which it was parked, a secondhand shop. It was a dirty, evil-looking, wretched little place that occupied the ground floor of an old brick building. Through the bleary windowpane she saw a miscellaneous assortment of shabby articles, old violins, rusty rifles, tattered books, old-fashioned cameras, pictures that might have been family heirlooms—a display that could be classified instantly as junk. Over the dark doorway a sign creaked in the autumn wind. In crude lettering she saw the name:

"Garbone."

Mr. Garbone, whoever he was, evidently thought that was enough, for he had dispensed with any advertisement of his place of business, and had even omitted his own initials.

"Well," said Jean to herself, "that car is parked in front of the store, so the man who drove it must be in the shop. What better place to sell a stolen lamp than in a secondhand shop?"

Without a moment's hesitation she opened the door and stepped into Mr. Garbone's shabby and sinister place of business. A bell tinkled overhead as she entered.

The place was very dark, for little light filtered in through the dirty windowpane and Mr. Garbone evidently economized on electricity. When Jean's eyes became accustomed to the gloom she found herself in a small wilderness of tumbledown chairs, sofas, kitchen tables, and other furniture, while on shelves behind the narrow counter were stacked more of the guns, cameras, watches, and other articles in which Mr. Garbone specialized. She wondered if he ever sold anything. Certainly she did not see a single article in the store that she would have accepted as a gift.

No one answered the tinkling bell, so Jean rapped firmly on the counter. Almost immediately she heard an oily voice:

"Yes, Lady? Is there anything I can do for you today?"

Silently a man had entered from some hidden recess at the back of the shop. He was a stout, swarthy individual with beetling eyebrows, dark eyes that glittered strangely, a nose like a beak, and a thin, cruel mouth. He rubbed his fat hands together as he moved stealthily behind the counter.

"Who is the owner of the car at your door?" asked Jean directly.

The man looked at her for a moment through half-closed eyes. Then he stepped gently to the window and looked out.

"The car at my door?" he murmured. "You wish to know the owner?"

"If you please."

The stout man rubbed his chin reflectively.

"As a matter of fact, Lady," he said, his cruel lips turning upward in what was meant to be a smile, "the car is mine. My name is Garbone. Jake Garbone, at your service."

Jean studied him for a moment. She disliked and distrusted the man at sight.

"Well, Mr. Garbone," she said, "I've come for the lamp you took from our house a little while ago. My name is Jean Dana."

Mr. Garbone frowned.

"What is this?" he said sharply. "What is this about a lamp? You say I took a lamp from your house?"

"If that is your car, I think you'd better give me an explanation." Jean's heart was thumping, but she stood her ground. "Someone entered our home and took a study lamp from the kitchen. The man drove away in a car with license number B7953. That's the license number of your car."

Mr. Garbone became violently angry.

"It is a lie!" he shouted. "I have not been out of my store all afternoon. I know nothing about a lamp. I am not a thief. I am an honest business man."

He came around the counter, advancing silently and menacingly on his rubber-heeled shoes.

"You will apologize to me for this insult," he rasped. "You come into my store and tell me I am a thief? What proof have you? Do you see this lamp anywhere in my store? Did you see me take it? Did you see me in the car? I tell you, that car has not been out of this street since noon. This is an outrage! I know nothing about it. You are an impudent girl.''

His eyes flamed with wrath. His face was harsh. Jean was momentarily frightened, but she did not quail.

"We followed that car all the way into Oak Falls,'' she said flatly.

"Not *that* car,'' stormed Garbone. "I tell you it has been in front of this store all afternoon. You have made a mistake.''

Doubt began to enter Jean's mind. She wondered if she had not made a ridiculous mistake after all in coming into this man's store and openly accusing him of stealing the lamp. Mr. Garbone's wrath did not seem feigned, and if he did not know anything about her uncle's gift, she felt that she could not blame him for losing his temper.

"Perhaps,'' she thought to herself, "I really ought to apologize.''

At that moment, over Mr. Garbone's shoulder, she saw something that brought a startled exclamation from her lips. The draperies at the back of the store parted slowly, and for a second there appeared a face. It was the white, sinister face of a woman with deep dark eyes, stringy black hair, and a cruel, painted mouth. She saw the features for but an instant; then they were gone.

Mr. Garbone glared at her and demanded: "What do you see?"

When he turned and followed the direction of Jean's frightened gaze, the evil-looking face had disappeared.

CHAPTER III

The Peril of the River

Louise was worried. She had searched through many streets without finding the robber's car. Now she was back at the Dana roadster, and there was no sign of Jean.

Louise, being of a more serious disposition than her gay, light-hearted sister, was prone to anxiety. She knew that Jean could not get lost in Oak Falls, but she was worried lest some harm had come to her in her search for the thief.

"It was foolish of me to let her go by herself," she thought.

She crossed the road and went into the part of the town where she had last seen her sister. Then she hesitated. What if Jean returned to the roadster in the meantime and went in search of *her?* She paused, undecided.

Then, to her overwhelming relief, she saw a familiar figure come hurrying around the corner. It was Jean. She rushed toward Louise, her eyes glowing, her cheeks flushed with excitement.

"Were you worrying about me?" she cried.

"Did you find the lamp?" asked Louise quickly.

"No, but I found the car."

"Where?"

"I'm sure it was the car. The license number was the same as the one you gave me." Jean was breathless as she told her story. "It was standing in front of a secondhand shop run by a man named Garbone. I went right into the store and accused him of stealing our lamp."

"You accused him!" exclaimed Louise, astonished.

"Why not? The car was there—and I didn't like the man's looks, anyway. He's just the sort of person who *would* steal the lamp."

"What did he say?"

"He was terribly angry," Jean laughed. "I thought he was going to throw me out of the store. He told me I had no proof. He denied being out of the shop, and said the car had been standing by the curb all afternoon. Do you know, for a minute or so I thought I had made a mistake. I was almost ready to apologize to him."

"But Jean, perhaps you did make a mistake. Maybe it wasn't his car after all."

"It was. He admitted it. And I'm sure of that license number. Louise, I think I would have apologized to him but for one thing."

"What was it?"

"I saw a face. It was a woman's face. She

looked through the draperies at the back of the shop. I saw her for only a few seconds —but Lou, there is something sinister about that shop. There's an atmosphere about it— well, I just *know* I'm right. That man Garbone stole our lamp."

"I'd like to see the secondhand shop," said Louise slowly.

"It isn't far. We'll walk past it and you can judge for yourself."

The two girls entered the narrow cross street and Jean guided her sister to the gloomy thoroughfare on which was located Mr. Jake Garbone's place of business. The moment Louise saw the license plate of the car she said decisively:

"That's the car. I would recognize it anywhere. You made no mistake there, Jean."

"I was sure I was right. But, just the same, Mr. Garbone was so angry—and when I saw that woman's face I was so frightened—I simply turned and walked out of the shop."

"What did she look like?"

"She had an evil face. Very white, with dank black hair and a painted mouth—horrible. And this man Garbone, he's fat and oily and greasy. I disliked him at sight."

The girls had reached the front of the store by now. Suddenly Jean gave a short scream.

"Her face—Louise——"

Louise looked into the window.

Beyond the bleary glass she saw a white face with deep-set, smouldering eyes, a red mouth, and sunken cheeks. It was there for only a moment. The eyes were fixed steadily upon her. Then the image vanished.

"Was that the woman?" she asked Jean in a hushed voice.

Jean nodded.

"Let's walk on. We don't want them to get too suspicious. I don't like that place."

The girls moved away and went out into the main street of Oak Falls. There they paused, undecided.

"Don't you think we should tell the police?" asked Jean.

Louise shook her head.

"No. If this mystery is solved at all, we'll solve it ourselves."

"What can we do?"

"Not very much at present, I'm afraid. But what can the police do? We haven't any proof that this man Garbone took the lamp."

"That," said Jean ruefully, "is what I realized when I accused him in the store. He knew I had no proof."

"Right now," said Louise, "I think we had better go home. If Garbone thinks he is suspected, he may become frightened and perhaps he'll see that we get the lamp back. In the meantime we'll try to figure out some sort of scheme."

The girls returned to the roadster. Louise glanced at her watch.

"Let's go back by the river road," she said. "We can call at Mrs. Daley's and bring Aunt Harriet home with us."

Louise had driven her relative out on the river road shortly after luncheon that afternoon to visit an old friend, and while it was probable that Mrs. Daley's son would volunteer to bring Aunt Harriet home, she decided that she might as well save him the trouble. Instead of continuing upon the main highway when they had crossed the bridge, therefore, she turned the car to the left and they followed the road that ran along the side of the stream.

Oak River was a rough, tumultuous body of water that ran swiftly between high, rocky shores that became sheer cliffs in many places. Turbulent rapids about half a mile above the town ended in the roaring cataract known as Oak Falls, a wild, fifty-foot plunge of foaming water. As the girls passed the falls they could hear their heavy, unending roar and see the mist of fine spray that hung above the river.

Beyond the falls the road skirted the bank closely, and only a few feet of shrubbery lay between the highway and the sharp declivity that ended in the long stretch of rapids.

"I don't see why a strong fence hasn't been built along this stretch of road," said Louise, steering carefully. "If anyone should lose control of his car along here—," she shuddered. "Why, he'd be down the bank and into the rapids in no time."

When they reached Mrs. Daley's place, they found that their aunt had already left. There was nothing to do, then, but to return home by way of the river road.

A short distance above the rapids they saw a man and a dog on the road ahead. Louise sounded the horn, but instead of stepping to one side the man turned and held up his arm. The dog, a handsome chow, capered about and barked, straining at his leash.

The stranger, a good-looking, slender fellow of about thirty-five, was dressed in a gray suit of excellent cut. His face was pleasant, and as Louise brought the car to a stop at the side of the road, he removed his hat, smiling.

"I'm sorry to trouble you," he said, "but I'm afraid my sense of direction isn't as good as it has been."

"Can we help you?" said Louise. She heard the rumble of a truck coming swiftly around the curve.

"Yes," replied the stranger. "I'm on my way to Captain Ned Dana's home. Could you tell me where to find it?"

"Why," exclaimed Jean, in surprise, "that's exactly where we're going——"

Suddenly she broke off with a scream.

The truck had come racing around the curve.

At the same instant the stranger's dog, with
a furious bark, broke from his leash. He
scampered out into the middle of the road,
directly in the path of the oncoming vehicle.

The traveler uttered a cry of alarm and
sprang toward the animal, but he was too late.
The chow, bewildered, tried to leap out of the
way of the speeding truck. There was a sharp
yelp of agony, a small, furry bundle went
hurtling through the air, and then the big machine flashed past. The girls had a glimpse
of the driver's face, as he bent over the wheel,
put on more speed, and vanished from sight.

The dog had been struck with such force that
it was thrown clear of the road. Horrified,
the onlookers heard a crackling and smashing
among the bushes on the steep bank above the
rapids, then another yelp and a distant splash.

The stranger's face was white.

"He's been killed!" he shouted, and raced
across the road. At the top of the bank he
did not hesitate.

"Look out!" cried Louise in warning. "It's
very steep."

The fringe of bushes beside the road had
deceived the man, who did not realize that they
hid a sharp, perilous drop to the river's edge.
He stood there for a moment, scrambling wildly
as he realized his danger. Then he lost his
balance, stumbled, and disappeared over the
edge of the embankment.

The girls scrambled hastily out of the car. They reached the top of the bank at the same moment. Down below they heard a hoarse cry of fear, the frenzied barking of the dog, the snapping and crackling of broken brush as the man plunged helplessly toward the water.

Out in the rushing torrent they could see the animal. He was swimming desperately against the current, trying to fight his way ashore.

As the girls stood there aghast, they noticed the man totter for a moment at the water's edge. He could not regain his balance, and with a wild cry he shot forward into the rapids.

"He'll be drowned! He'll be swept over the falls!" screamed Jean.

She did not hesitate. Quickly she began to climb down the steep embankment. Louise, whose mind worked swiftly, turned and ran back to the roadster.

There was not a moment to lose. Both man and dog faced the terrible fate of being swept over Oak Falls.

CHAPTER IV

A Cry for Help

Out of the back of the roadster Louise hastily snatched a length of stout rope that had been kept there for emergency. She was back at the top of the embankment again before Jean was halfway to the water's edge.

Out in the stream the dog was still fighting valiantly against the current, trying with all his feeble strength to make his way to safety. As for the man, he had disappeared.

Louise's heart sank. For a moment she was sure the stranger had been drowned. Then, as she made her way hurriedly down the bushy slope, regardless of the undergrowth that clawed at her stockings and tore a great rent in her skirt, she saw a limp, motionless form come swirling out of a smother of foam and dancing water, to be flung violently against two jagged rocks that rose above the turmoil of the rapids.

The man was unconscious, probably having struck his head against a rock when he had tumbled into the river. Now the current had picked him up and was drawing him ir-

resistibly downstream. Jean had reached the
shore by now, but she was standing there
uncertainly, powerless to give help.

Fortunately for the stranger, the current
that had washed him against the rocks now
held him there. He was wedged partly between
two boulders and was held there as if in a
vise. The waves crashed against him. Now
the limp body was hidden by a swirling rush
of water, now it lay there against the rocks,
clearly revealed to the horrified girls.

Jean ran down the bank a little distance,
seeing that the dog was now close to shore.
The animal had given up fighting the current
and had allowed himself to be swept downstream, at the same time swimming toward
shore. The dog had thus gained in its progress.
But Jean saw that it would reach the bank
at a place where the rocks rose sheer to a distance of several feet from the edge of the water
and where there was no chance of gaining a
foothold.

She reached the steep acclivity just as the
dog came paddling in against the rocks. Whimpering, the poor animal tried to scramble out
of the water, but its paws slipped against the
smooth surface and it fell back. Jean flung
herself down upon the rocks and reached desperately toward the struggling creature. At
first her straining fingers missed as the dog
was being gradually forced away by the cur-

rent, but by a magnificent effort it turned and fought its way slowly back with its last vestige of strength. Jean's fingers closed about its furry coat, she dragged it closer, seized it by the collar, and finally drew it out of the water.

Louise was calling to her.

"Jean! Hurry!"

Swiftly the older sister was knotting one end of the rope around her waist. Oak River, at the rapids, was not very deep. On this fact alone she based her hope of rescuing the stranger from the grip of the river, although she knew that the hope was slight. She realized that the risk would be great, yet she did not hesitate. It would be only a matter of moments before the unconscious man on the rocks would be slowly drowned by the successive waves that crashed over him as he lay wedged in the rocky trap. Either that, or the undertow would drag him free and send his body hurtling toward the falls below.

The dog lay on the rocks panting, feebly trying to wag its tail to show some gratitude. Jean picked herself up and ran back to where her sister was standing. She took in the situation at a glance.

"Louise!" she gasped. "You can't—you can't go out there!"

"We can't stand here and watch him drown," returned Louise. "No, I'm going to try it. Why, it's our only chance of saving the man.''

"But you may be swept over the falls yourself.''

"I'll have to take that chance.'' Louise's nimble fingers knotted the rope firmly. "I'm going to try to wade out to him. If you'll hold the rope and let it out slowly, I may be able to reach him.''

Before Jean could object further, Louise thrust the end of the rope into her sister's hands, then turned and stepped into the rushing water.

The current swept her off her feet in a twinkling and she was struggling in the river. Jean, clinging to the rope, was almost dragged off her feet by the sudden shock, but she braced herself, held the hemp firmly, and then saw that Louise was fighting her way slowly but indomitably toward the figure against the rocks.

She paid out the rope, holding it tight when the current threatened to drag Louise out of her course, releasing it when Louise forged ahead. In the shallow water the rescuer was able to reach the shelter of a group of rocks that broke the force of the stream, and from there she waded knee-deep in swirling foam until she was only a few yards from the unconscious man.

Then Jean gasped with horror. The figure against the rocks had shifted.

The body had sagged to one side and slipped down the face of the boulders; it was no longer wedged securely between the rocks. One more buffeting impact by a wave and it would be washed clear—washed out into the roaring current of mid-river.

She screamed to Louise, warning her of the danger. But Louise had already seen the sagging movement of the limp form. She splashed out from the shelter of the rocky barrier, flung herself into the water, and let the current sweep her directly toward the helpless man.

She was just in the nick of time. Scarcely had her hands gripped his clothing than the motionless form slipped down from between the rocks. In another moment he would have been swept out into the stream. Louise clung tightly to him, braced herself against the boulders for a second, then turned. She shouted something, but above the steady roar of the river Jean could not distinguish the words. She knew, however, that Louise was about to essay the perilous return journey.

Jean clung to the rope, hauled steadily as Louise began her battle with the current. When she saw that her sister was clear of the boulders she released the tension a little. As in the case of the dog, the current swept both the man and his rescuer downstream, but with the stout cord acting as a check, Jean was able to aid her sister's progress inshore. Inch by inch she paid out the rope, gathering in the slack whenever there was a moment's respite against the current's drag.

Finally, utterly exhausted and gasping with weariness, Louise stumbled in toward the shore, dragging her helpless and unconscious burden.

"Thank goodness!" breathed Jean, weak with relief, as she sprang forward to help her sister out of the water. The dog, when it saw its master being carried gently ashore, came up barking feebly.

The man lay senseless on the bank. There was an ugly bruise on his left temple and for a moment the girls were afraid he was beyond help. His heart was still beating, however, so they did their best to bring him back to consciousness.

Their efforts, however, were in vain.

"We'll have to get him to a doctor," decided Louise quickly. "He may have fractured his skull."

"We'll take him home. He was trying to find his way there anyway. Perhaps Aunt Harriet will know who he is."

Between them they managed to drag and carry the stranger up the embankment. Whimpering, the dog scampered ahead. With difficulty they lifted their burden into the roadster, and in a few minutes were speeding homeward.

Their arrival created a sensation. Aunt

Harriet, who was busy in the kitchen making
preparations for a farewell party to her nieces
that evening, was almost dumbfounded when
they struggled into the house, wet and be-
draggled, carrying the unconscious man, with
a drenched and dispirited looking dog close at
their heels.

As for Cora Appel, she simply gaped and
exclaimed, "Well, I never!" very emphatically,
and dropped a pan of cookies with a tremendous clatter.

Aunt Harriet took command of the situation
instantly when the two girls breathlessly told
her what had happened. The stranger was
still unconscious and breathing heavily.

"Put him in the spare room!" ordered Aunt
Harriet. She called for Ben Harrow, the hired
man, and instructed him to carry the stranger
upstairs. "Louise, you're simply drenched.
You had better change into dry clothes at once
or you'll catch pneumonia. Cora, pick up those
cookies and stop snivelling. Jean, get one of
your uncle's nightgowns and a dressing gown
out of his room. Ben, when you take the man
upstairs, get him out of those wet clothes right
away."

"Wh-wh-what happened, M-m-miss?" asked
Ben. "W-w-was he s-s-s-swimming?"

"He fell into the river. The girls will tell
us all about it later. Get busy now, everyone.
I'm going to call the doctor."

The Dana home was a scene of unprecedented
excitement and confusion for the next few
hours. The physician who came from Oak
Falls explained that the unexpected and unconscious guest was not seriously injured and
that he might be expected to recover his senses
at any time.

"His skull isn't fractured, as I feared," said
the doctor. "He got a bad bump and he's still
dead to the world, but he'll come around all
right. If he is still unconscious after a few
hours, let me know."

As he was leaving, the man of medicine
turned to Aunt Harriet and said:

"By the way, what's the man's name?"

"I haven't the slightest idea," returned Miss
Dana. "According to the girls, he stopped
their car and asked the way to our home, just
before the accident. But he's a stranger
to me."

"Odd," said the doctor, and departed.

Preparations for the party planned for the
eve of the girls' return to Starhurst School
had been thrown into confusion, and now they
were resumed in a frantic, last-minute attempt
to restore order out of chaos. Up in their
room Louise and Jean hurriedly donned the
dainty dresses that had been specially ordered
for the occasion. Ten guests were due to arrive at eight o'clock and half-past seven found
the house still in an uproar.

"My slippers!" wailed Jean, looking under the bed. "I can't find my slippers."

"There they are behind the door. But where —*where* is my nail file?" gasped Louise, greatly flurried. "We'll never be ready in time."

Down in the kitchen Aunt Harriet was like a general on the field of battle. Cora Appel was so confused and excited that she performed feats of stupidity almost impossible of belief.

"Seven years' bad luck," she muttered, as she stumbled away from the china cabinet with the sugar bowl. "I've never known it to fail. The minute I broke that lookin' glass I knew we were in for it. And here's a half-dead stranger in the house already, and everything upset, and the people will be comin' in the front door before I know where I'm at."

"Fill the sugar bowl, Cora," said Aunt Harriet, "and stop that nonsensical talk or you'll have the bad luck to be looking for another place."

Thereupon Cora burst into tears and lamentations, and desolately declared that she was doing the best she could, that she hadn't a friend in the world, and that a poor girl with only one pair of hands couldn't be expected to do umpteen dozen things at one and the same time.

Miraculously, however, under Aunt Harriet's deft management, order was restored, and by the time the first guests arrived, Jean and Louise were in the hall to meet them, and the household was at peace.

Five boys and five girls, all friends of Louise and Jean, had been invited for the evening. For a time the shadow that overhung the household in the presence of the unconscious figure upstairs was forgotten. To be sure, Cora Appel was so flustered and nervous that Aunt Harriet was driven to distraction in the kitchen by the maid's errors—salt in the sugar bowl, sugar in the salt cellars, coffee in the teapot, and the ice cream placed absent-mindedly on the back of the stove. These accidental manifestations of "Applecore's" incurable stupidity were remedied before any damage was done, however, and the evening passed pleasantly.

The Oak Falls friends of the Dana girls were genuinely sorry that the sisters were leaving, for they were popular and well-liked by the young people of the town.

"Not that I don't envy you," admitted Sally Gray, a pretty, brown-haired lass of fifteen summers. "I wish I were going to Starhurst. You get such lovely long vacations. But it's back to dear old Oak Falls High for me——"

"What's the matter with Oak Falls High?" demanded Sam Gray, her brother, halfback of the school football team.

"Nothing," shrugged his sister, "except that it has too many boys in it. For myself, I'd rather go to a school where there aren't any."

"So far as I'm concerned, a school full of girls is my idea of a mighty tame place," sniffed Sam.

"You don't know Starhurst," laughed Jean. "Now just you listen to me, Sam Gray——"

Jean's defense of Starhurst was never uttered, for at that moment there was a surprising interruption. From the upper regions of the house came a shrill, frantic scream.

"Help! Help!"

The cry was followed by a sickening thud!

CHAPTER V

Franklin Starr

"What's that?" cried Louise, startled.

The guests sprang to their feet. From the kitchen came a shriek from Cora Appel.

"I knew it! I knew it! I just knew them seven years of bad luck would start right away. There's been murder done in this house. That poor man upstairs is bein' killed."

From the second floor came sounds of thudding and banging, another strangled cry. It appeared that a lively fight was in progress.

"What *can* have happened?" gasped Aunt Harriet.

"I'm going to find out," said Louise with determination. She ran into the hall, closely followed by Jean.

"Don't go!" clamored Cora Appel, peeping through the kitchen doorway. "You'll be killed, sure."

"Nonsense!" snapped Louise. She switched on the light and ran up the stairs. In the guest room the uproar continued. Crash! A chair had tumbled over. "Help!" roared a stentorian voice.

"Why, that voice is familiar!" exclaimed Jean, as Louise sped into the room, and in a moment had flashed on the lights.

On the floor rolled two men, struggling desperately. Panting and puffing, they were clinging to each other, rolling against the bed, against the bureau, crashing into the wall.

One of the men was the stranger, now in full possession of his senses. The other, to the unbounded surprise of the girls, was Captain Ned Dana!

"Uncle Ned!" exclaimed Louise.

The two gladiators parted, rolled free of each other, and sat up, breathing heavily. They glared at each other. The stranger blinked and suddenly looked very foolish. Gingerly he rubbed a bruise beneath his eye.

"Captain Dana!" he muttered.

Uncle Ned stared at him.

"Well, I'll be hornswoggled!" he bellowed. "It's Franklin Starr! What in time are *you* doing here?"

"What does it mean?" asked Louise, completely mystified. "What are you fighting about? Uncle Ned—how did you get into the house? We didn't expect you until tomorrow."

Aunt Harriet now appeared in the hallway.

"Well, this is a fine homecoming!" she said. "What's been going on?"

Franklin Starr got to his feet.

"I'm very sorry," he said. "I'm afraid it

was all my fault." He looked about him uncertainly. "I don't know where I am, or how I got here—the last I remember was being in the river—but I awoke from a nightmare and I heard someone in the room, so I tackled him."

Captain Dana, bluff, red-faced, and sturdy, looked very sheepish.

"The fact is," he said, "I managed to get out of New York sooner than I expected, and when I got home and saw there was a party going on—why, I thought I'd better sneak quietly upstairs and change my clothes and surprise everybody."

"You did!" Aunt Harriet assured him grimly.

"I—I'm very sorry," faltered Franklin Starr. "I'm really to blame for the rumpus. Not knowing where I was, and suddenly waking up to hear someone in the room—why, I'm afraid I've caused a great deal of trouble."

He looked so apologetic that Aunt Harriet hastened to put him at his ease.

"It's quite all right," she assured him. "But you and Captain Dana seem to be friends."

"You bet we're friends," declared Uncle Ned. "Franklin Starr has crossed the Atlantic with me half a dozen times. One of my best customers, you might say. He promised to give me a dog——"

"I brought it with me." Then Franklin

Starr looked alarmed. "At least I hope so."
His face was puzzled. "I still can't understand how I came to be here. How did I get
out of the river? Is the dog safe?"

"Let's get this all straightened out," said
Captain Dana. "I'm in the dark, too. I come
home to find Franklin Starr in the house and
I don't know how he got here. Neither does
he. What's the mystery?"

Aunt Harriet laughed. She introduced Jean
and Louise to Mr. Starr.

"They fished you out of the river," she explained. "The dog, I'm glad to say, is quite
safe. He's asleep in the kitchen right now.
If you and Ned will come downstairs and meet
the guests, we'll tell you the whole story."

"Wait until I get into my shore clothes,"
begged Captain Ned. "I don't want to miss
this."

Within a short time Captain Ned and Franklin Starr had made themselves presentable and
had been introduced to the guests at the party.
Then Aunt Harriet told the story of the rescue.
Both Jean and Louise modestly disclaimed any
special credit, but when Mr. Starr learned that
they had been responsible, he insisted upon
shaking hands with them warmly.

"I can remember how ugly those rapids
looked," he said. "Just before I hit my head
on a rock I had given up all hope."

"You waded into Oak Falls Rapids?" spluttered Captain Ned. "With a rope? And you brought him ashore?" He regarded his nieces with admiration. "Well, by the Great Horn Spoon, all I can say is that there're plenty of men who wouldn't have done it."

"I was quite safe," laughed Louise. "There really wasn't any danger as long as the rope didn't break."

"No danger!" sniffed Captain Ned.

"It was a mighty good stunt—for a girl," admitted Sam Gray.

"For a girl? For anybody!" declared Franklin Starr.

It was not until after the guests had left at the conclusion of the party that night, that the family learned more about their guest. Captain Ned explained that he had made the acquaintance of Starr on board the *Balaska* several years previously. Mr. Starr had crossed the Atlantic a number of times since then and they had become good friends.

"On my last trip," explained Franklin Starr, "the Captain remarked that he had always wanted to own a dog, so I promised that I would bring him one. I was on my way to the house with the pet when I met the girls on the road."

"Well," grunted Captain Ned, "you certainly got introduced to the family mighty thoroughly. Lucky you weren't killed. How's your head?"

Franklin Starr rubbed the bruise on his temple.

"It's sore yet. I daresay I'll be all right in a day or so."

"What's the idea of the party tonight?" demanded the captain, looking at his sister.

"Have you forgotten? The girls are leaving for Starhurst tomorrow."

Captain Ned slapped his knee.

"I'd clean forgotten!" he exclaimed. "Back to school again, eh? I won't see much of my nieces this trip."

"Starhurst?" said Franklin Starr questioningly.

"My nieces go to the Starhurst School for Girls," explained Aunt Harriet. "This will be their sophomore year."

Franklin Starr smiled.

"You know my sister, then?" he said. "She has been at Starhurst for the past two years."

"Not Evelyn Starr!" they exclaimed in delight.

"Why, we know her quite well," said Louise.

"Oh, now I remember!" Jean exclaimed. "Didn't Evelyn live at Starhurst before—well, before it became a school at all?"

Franklin Starr nodded. His face was grave.

"The place takes its name from the Starr family," he said. "My grandfather built Starhurst. Evelyn and I spent our childhood there, but after our parents died—and one thing after another happened, the family fortunes failed, and so——"

"You had to sell the place?" asked Captain Ned sympathetically.

"Yes, we had to let it go. Mr. and Mrs. Crandall bought it and transformed it into a school for girls."

"What a shame," said Jean warmly. "It's the most wonderful old place. I can imagine what a lovely home it must have been."

"Really too large for us," said Franklin Starr. "It was an expensive luxury, although naturally we were deeply attached to it."

"By the way," remarked Uncle Ned, "where's that lamp I sent you girls? Hope you don't mind my changing the subject, Starr, but I sent the girls a little present yesterday and they haven't mentioned it yet, so I've been wondering if it got here at all."

There was an awkward silence.

"Didn't it come?" demanded Uncle Ned.

"Yes—it came," added Louise.

"And went," added Jean.

"It was stolen," explained Aunt Harriet.

"But what—how—I don't understand this!" spluttered the captain, greatly upset. "The lamp couldn't have reached here before this afternoon——"

"It wasn't in the house ten minutes before it was stolen," Louise assured him.

Uncle Ned leaped from his chair, agitated,

and began to pace up and down the room as if he were back on his own ship's bridge. "Stolen?" he fumed. "That's a fine how-d' ye-do. Mean to say somebody walked right into the house and took it? Why, that lamp—!" He checked himself. "How did it happen, Louise?" he asked in a gentler voice.

Louise told him the whole story, explained how they had left the lamp unguarded in the kitchen when Cora Appel broke the mirror, and told how they had seen the mysterious car disappearing down the driveway.

"A thief in a car!" snorted the captain. "I must say he didn't lose any time. Must have followed the express driver out here. Did you get the number of the car?"

"Not only that," Louise told him, "but we followed it to Oak Falls and then Jean found the car parked in front of a secondhand shop."

"And I'm just positive," declared Jean, "that the secondhand dealer is the man who stole that lamp. His name is Jake Garbone and he's a dreadful person." She told them about her visit to the secondhand shop and her interview with Garbone.

"So!" said Captain Ned grimly. "And he denied takin' the lamp, eh? We'll see about that. First thing tomorrow I'm going to Oak Falls, and if I don't shake the truth out of Jake Garbone, I'm not worthy of my name."

"And I'll go with you!" said Franklin Starr,

CHAPTER VI

THE GYPSYLIKE WOMAN

UNCLE NED was upset over the theft of the study lamp. There was no doubt about that. When the Dana girls came down to breakfast the next morning, they found the bluff captain determined and eager to set out without delay in search of the gift.

"We'll find it!" he growled. "I'll take that fellow Garbone by the scruff of the neck and shake the truth out of him, so I will."

Franklin Starr, a little pale but looking refreshed after his night's rest, rose and bowed as the girls came into the room.

"Your uncle is trying to persuade me to go out on a man hunt with him," he smiled. "Or perhaps I should call it a lamp hunt."

"You'll come with me, Starr," said the captain. "No nonsense about it. We'll go to this secondhand shop and we'll get—that—lamp!"

Uncle Ned emphasized this statement, word for word, by pounding the table with his huge fist.

"We'll come, too," said Louise.

The captain shook his head.

"You're leaving for Starhurst this afternoon. You'll be too busy."

"Not too busy to help look for our own present," replied Jean. "You can't keep us out of this, Uncle Ned. Besides, we've finished our packing—almost. We have the whole morning before us."

"All right, all right," grunted Uncle Ned. "But I don't hold with girls getting mixed up in these affairs. This is a man's job."

"I daresay we could solve the mystery of this lamp quite as well as any man," declared Jean. "I think we'd make good detectives if we had a chance."

Uncle Ned wagged his head and winked at Franklin Starr.

"There's the modern girl for you, Mr. Starr," he said. "Think they can do anything. It's not a man's world any more. I tell you, it won't surprise me if one of these days I find a hard-bitten old lady in spectacles and a plaid shawl standing on the bridge when I step up to take the *Balaska* on another run. 'I'm the new skipper,' she'll say. And I'll say, 'I knew something like this would happen, but I didn't expect it in my lifetime.' And then I'll have to come home and spend the rest of my days raising chickens."

The girls laughed.

"It won't be as bad as all that, Uncle Ned," soothed Louise. "And of course we have no

intention of going into business as private detectives when we leave Starhurst. But I think
you'd better let us come along with you this
morning.''

"I see myself trying to keep you at home,"
laughed Uncle Ned.

They were all due for a disappointment,
however. When they drove in to Oak Falls
after breakfast, with Uncle Ned breathing fire
and brimstone and explaining what he would
do to Jake Garbone when they met face to face,
they went directly to the secondhand shop.

It was closed. The door was locked.

Uncle Ned rattled the latch, banged on the
door, even kicked it. He peered through the
grimy window.

"No luck?" inquired Franklin Starr.

"He knew we'd be after him," growled the
captain, disappointed. "He cleared out, that's
what he did. Closed up his shop, the scoundrel."

The girls were quite as disappointed as their
uncle, as they had looked forward to a clash
between Captain Ned and the oily Garbone.
However, there was nothing to be gained by
staring at the uncommunicative window of the
secondhand shop.

"If you don't mind," said Franklin Starr,
as they were about to drive away, "I think
I'll drop off at the railroad station."

The captain stared at him.

"Why? You're not going away, are you?"

Starr pressed his hand to his temple. A spasm of pain contorted his face.

"I have a terrible headache," he confessed. "I'm afraid I'll have to leave here by an early train."

"Oh, but you can't do that," protested Uncle Ned. "I thought you were going to stay with me for a week or so."

Franklin Starr smiled.

"I'm sorry, Captain, but that would be impossible. There are certain matters—business affairs—no, I think I had better go to the station and get my ticket. If this headache keeps up, I won't be very good company for anyone, I assure you."

The captain grumbled that everyone seemed bent on spoiling his holiday. Although he did his best to persuade Franklin Starr to remain at the Dana home for a few days, he could not overcome the guest's sudden and insistent determination to leave at once. Jean and Louise were puzzled. The young man had been walking to their home when they had met him, he had brought no luggage, and now he was vague as to his destination.

There was a crowd of people on the station platform when they arrived at the depot, for the morning express had pulled in. Franklin Starr, however, seemed to be in no hurry.

"Is that your train?" asked the captain.

"Well—no—I don't think so," returned Mr. Starr, as he got out of the roadster. "I think I'll just get my ticket."

He wandered off down the platform and was soon lost in the crowd. Uncle Ned frowned.

"Always was a queer sort of chap," he muttered, "but I never knew him to act like this before. Maybe that blow on the head hurt him more than we think."

Franklin Starr returned in a few minutes, a railroad ticket in his hand. The express was just about to leave. The conductor sang out, "All ab—oard!" The bell of the locomotive clanged.

"I think," said Starr, "I'll wait around until the next train. It will be along in about ten minutes or so——"

At that moment a short, stout man bustled out of the waiting room and ran across the platform. A surprising change came across Franklin Starr's face. He gave a slight gasp.

"Why, there he is—I mean—that's the fellow I'm looking for!" he exclaimed, and without another word he hurried away.

"It's Mr. Garbone!" cried Jean.

It was, indeed, the proprietor of the second-hand shop. The train was already in motion and Mr. Garbone was scrambling up the steps. Jean sprang out of the roadster.

"What?" bellowed Uncle Ned. "The fellow who stole the lamp?"

He jumped out onto the platform, but there was no hope of detaining Mr. Garbone in conversation just then. The train was picking up speed rapidly—so rapidly, in fact, that although Franklin Starr ran along the platform for a few yards, apparently trying to pluck up sufficient courage to board the express, he changed his mind. Within a few seconds the last of the coaches had glided past. Mr. Starr gazed after the receding train for a moment, then turned and almost blundered into Jean as the others came hurrying up.

"It was Mr. Garbone, the secondhand man!" she cried. "Do you know him?"

"Garbone?" said Starr blankly.

"Yes. The stout man. The man you were looking for."

"Oh! Was *that* Garbone?" asked Starr. He appeared upset and bewildered. "Why— I must have made a mistake. I thought he was a man I knew——"

He offered no further explanation of his strange conduct.

There was a mystery about Franklin Starr; of that the girls were convinced. He still insisted that he would wait at the station for the next train, murmured something about being obliged to see his lawyer at once, but made no further reference to his recognition of Jake Garbone. When they finally left him on the platform and drove back home, the Danas agreed that his conduct had been, to say the least, peculiar.

The incidents of the morning, however, were soon forgotten in the bustle and flurry of packing when they reached the house. Jean had been optimistic in her assertion that their packing was completed, for a score of last-minute preparations still remained. By the time lunch was over, the trunks opened and locked again for the last time, the hatboxes and hand luggage inspected by Aunt Harriet, everyone was exhausted. "Applecore" was in tears and did not add to the joy of the occasion by her prediction that the train would doubtless be wrecked.

"Seven years of bad luck," she mourned, "and not a full day of it gone yet. I don't know how I'm going to face it all by myself."

Finally, however, the farewells were made and the Dana girls drove away with Uncle Ned. As the car turned onto the highway they could see Aunt Harriet standing very straight and stern in the doorway, but with eyes glistening with tears, with "Applecore" weeping into her apron, and Ben Harrow leaning against the fence, chewing reflectively at a straw. Not until Christmas would they return to the old home——

"But Starhurst lies ahead!" cried Jean gaily, voicing her sister's unspoken thought.

They passed through the streets of Oak Falls,

bound for the station. It was while the car was
held up for a moment at an intersection that
the strange affair of the stolen lamp was recalled in startling fashion. A taxi, also waiting for the green light, drew up alongside.
Jean suddenly gripped her sister's arm.

"Louise! Look! The woman!"

Startled, her sister turned.

Through the window of the taxicab she got
a momentary glimpse of a white, evil face—
the face of a woman with dark, smouldering
eyes. They were the same eyes she had seen
peering through the window of Jake Garbone's
secondhand shop, the very ones which had spied
on Jean through the draperies.

Then the face disappeared as the woman
sank back into the shadows of the cab. The
signal light changed, the traffic moved on, and
the car lurched ahead.

Louise turned to her sister.

"The same woman!"

Jean nodded. "Horrible looking creature!
She gives me the creeps."

The incident had not been noticed by Uncle
Ned, who was at the wheel and had been intent
on the business of driving at the moment. They
said nothing to him about the affair, for after
all the mere fact that they had seen her in
Jake Garbone's shop meant little. When they
reached the station, however, they were surprised to see her already on the platform.

She was a gypsylike creature in her flashy, colorful clothes, and she wore a dozen strings of beads around her neck, while her wrists and fingers were covered with cheap bracelets and rings. Her dark eyes flashed as she looked insolently at the girls while she sauntered up and down.

"Perhaps," reflected Louise, "she's waiting to meet Jake Garbone. He may be coming back on this train."

"Well, good-bye, Chicks," Uncle Ned was saying. "Be sure to write often to your Aunt Harriet. And drop me a line once in a while when you have time. I'm sorry you haven't your present to take with you, but you know my intentions were good, anyway."

"We know that, Uncle Ned," they told him warmly. "You mustn't worry about it."

The train was pulling in. Uncle Ned kissed his two nieces. Shrill cries from a group of girls in one of the coaches attracted their attention as the train came to a stop. Crowded in two of the windows they saw the gay, welcoming faces of four of their Starhurst chums. Uncle Ned beamed.

"You'll have company to Penfield," he said.

The gypsylike woman, who was standing a few paces away, muttered to herself:

"Yes, you'll have company to Penfield."

CHAPTER VII

BACK AT STARHURST

NELL CARSON, Doris Harland, Ann Freeman, and Margaret Glenn, the other Starhurst girls who were returning to Penfield by the same train, greeted the Dana girls with shouts of glee. Flushed with excitement and chattering like magpies, they made a gay party as the train resumed its journey. Everyone tried to talk at once as they related their vacation experiences, discussed plans for the coming semester, and exchanged news about their other chums.

"Margaret and I are going to room together," said Doris.

Louise had noticed that the gypsylike woman had seated herself across the aisle, but paid no attention as she spoke to her friends.

"Uncle Ned gave us the loveliest present for our study," she told the others. "It was a lamp. A beautiful antique lamp."

There was a chorus of appreciation. "Where is it? May we see it when you unpack? What color is the shade?" These and many other questions were hurled at Louise.

"We didn't bring it with us," said Jean soberly. "As a matter of fact, we didn't have the lamp for more than five or ten minutes."

"You broke it!" declared Nell Carson, shocked.

Louise shook her head.

"It was stolen. It was stolen ten minutes after we unwrapped it."

The Dana girls told their chums the whole story. They did not, however, relate the tale of the search. Louise glanced at the gypsylike passenger from time to time to see whether the conversation was being noticed, but the woman's expression was calm and she did not seem to be at all disturbed.

"Well," said Ann Freeman indignantly, "I think it's a downright shame. Why didn't you tell the police?"

"We thought we would try to find it ourselves," said Jean.

"You won't find it at Starhurst," laughed Doris.

"Uncle Ned is taking up the search. We think we know who stole the lamp," said Louise, watching the stranger out of the corner of her eye, "and if Uncle Ned doesn't find it, he'll probably notify the authorities."

The bejeweled traveler got up suddenly and made her way down the aisle. After a while the girls saw her in earnest conversation with a woman who sat alone in a seat midway down the coach. She produced a pack of cards and spread them out on an upturned suitcase.

"Oh, she must be a fortune teller!" exclaimed Margaret.

The middle-aged lady to whom the flashily dressed gypsy stranger was talking seemed to be highly absorbed in the revelations of the cards. At a command from the other she placed her purse on top of the suitcase, and the mind reader covered it with a scarlet silk handkerchief, meanwhile talking rapidly.

"Fortune telling!" thought Louise contemptuously. "She'll probably rob her client."

For a time the girls dismissed the woman from their minds. When the train finally reached Penfield, however, the Dana girls were surprised to see that the gypsylike person was also getting off the train. Suddenly Jean nudged her sister.

"Louise! She's taking that woman's suitcase."

The fortune teller was hastily leaving the train with the suitcase belonging to the middle-aged lady, having taken it from the pile of luggage which had been put in the vestibule by the porter. The victim of the barefaced theft had not yet realized her loss, for she was absent-mindedly adjusting her coat, apparently serene in her conviction that the porter was looking after her baggage.

The thief hurried off down the platform.

Louise did not hesitate a moment, but ran after her and touched her arm.

"I beg your pardon," she said, "but I think you have made a mistake."

The woman turned, her eyes flashing.

"A mistake?" she asked harshly. "What do you mean, girl?"

"You have taken the wrong suitcase, haven't you?" asked Louise firmly.

"This is my suitcase!"

"I'm quite sure it belongs to that lady who is just getting off the train."

At that moment the middle-aged woman discovered her loss and began to expostulate with the porter. That worthy was staring blankly at the luggage on the platform, counting the various pieces over and over, and scratching his head in bewilderment.

"No, lady," he was saying, "I didn't see no suitcase like what you say. Mus' be in dat coach yet——"

"But you put the suitcases in the vestibule! I saw you."

The porter looked helpless.

"How stupid of me!" declared the gypsy woman suddenly. "This one looks so much like my own—I never thought—" She flounced back and seized her own property. "It's all your fault, porter!" she snapped, and hurried into the station.

"Caught red-handed!" murmured Louise.

They restored the bag to the woman, vastly to her relief.

"I should have been in a terrible fix without it," she said gratefully. "I'm sure that woman tried to steal it. Fortune telling, indeed! She told me to be on my guard against a dark-haired man. Dark-haired woman, she should have said."

She gave a calling card to the girls, which revealed that her name was Mrs. Grantland. Still volubly expressing her gratitude for the recovery of the suitcase, she hurried to a taxi, while the girls collected their luggage and boarded the bus for Starhurst School.

The charm of the Starhurst School for Girls, over which Mr. and Mrs. Crandall presided, lay in the fact that it did not resemble a school at all. The Starr family had been wealthy, and a great deal of money had been spent on the beautiful estate surrounding the old family mansion. Noble avenues of trees and sweeping expanses of lawn formed an imposing setting for a house that had grandeur and dignity in the aristocratic tradition.

Mr. and Mrs. Crandall personally greeted the girls when they arrived. Mr. Crandall was a tall, kindly man with silvery hair and a dreamy expression—a vague, impractical person who always appeared to be thinking of something far away. He had, however, a genius for teaching, and there was a school legend to the effect that his spare time was spent in the writing of a monumental work on Ancient Greece, destined to appear in five volumes, but Mr. Crandall had never been known to mention this work to anyone. The girls agreed, however, that it would account for his absent-minded manner.

Mrs. Crandall was the real head of the school. She was a tall, dignified woman, the soul of efficiency. She selected the students with care, taking pride in the reputation of the institution, and her management of the place was beyond reproach.

"I have some good news for you, girls," she told Jean and Louise when they were in her office.

"Do we—do we get the second-floor study?"

"I remember that you asked me for it when you were leaving at the end of the term, but I couldn't make any promise then. Yes, you may have it, and I hope you will find it comfortable."

"Oh, thank you, Mrs. Crandall!" they exclaimed. "It's the loveliest study in the whole school."

"Well, there are others I like quite as well myself," said the principal, "but you seem to have taken a fancy to it. I have assigned it to you, and the porter will put your trunks there as soon as they arrive."

The Dana girls were greatly pleased, as they had envied the occupants of that particular study during the previous term. The view, overlooking the grounds, was superb, and the room itself, panelled in old dark oak, had a huge fireplace. It had once been a library and had been designed for comfort. There was a big window seat, many shelves, odd nooks, and a hidden closet that could be opened only by pressing a spring in the panelling. The closet, of course, was no longer secret, as every girl at Starhurst had begged for the privilege of seeing it, but the mere possession of such a luxury was glory enough.

When the Dana girls left the office, they hurried to the prized study. The halls were full of chattering groups of girls, and Jean and Louise were halted frequently by welcoming friends. When they finally reached their new quarters, they were surprised to find the door open.

Jean's face fell.

"Surely Mrs. Crandall didn't make a mistake!" she said. "I hope someone else hasn't taken possession."

Then they heard a shrill voice.

"I've had my heart set on this study for a whole year and now I'm going to have it. We'll go down to see Mrs. Crandall at once."

The Dana girls halted outside the door, having recognized the voice. The speaker was Lettie Briggs, a tall, anaemic girl whose arrogant, snobbish manner had made her unpop ular at Starhurst from the day she had enrolled at the school. Lettie's parents were enormously wealthy, but her breeding was not such that she could permit the circumstance to go unmentioned. She lost no opportunity of grandly informing her schoolmates that her father had made his money in oil, and that he "could buy the whole place and use it for a garage if he so wished."

Lettie had one friend, Ina Mason, a meek, toadying sort of girl who was the veritable shadow of the spoiled daughter of wealth.

Now they heard Ina's voice:

"But I heard—someone was saying," she faltered, "that the Dana girls were to have this study."

"The Dana girls!" exclaimed Lettie shrilly. "They may *want* this study, but they won't get it. I'm going to Mrs. Crandall right away and tell her that I have decided to take it."

Louise nudged her sister. Quietly they entered the big, comfortable room. Lettie and Ina, who were standing in front of the great fireplace, whirled around.

"Greetings!" said Jean blithely as she tossed her hat onto the window seat. "Glad to see you back, Lettie. You're looking awfully well, Ina."

Ina replied with a frightened nod and glanced dubiously at Lettie Briggs. That young lady sniffed.

"What do you want?" she asked rudely.

"Why, nothing at all," returned Louise innocently. "Are you admiring our study?"

"*Your* study!" cried Lettie.

"Surely," said Jean. "Didn't you know? Mrs. Crandall assigned it to us. Aren't we lucky?"

"Lucky!" sniffed Miss Briggs. "I don't believe you were given this room. I have decided to move in here myself."

"Isn't that too bad?" said Louise. "Of course, we didn't *dream*——"

"Oh, no. Of course not!" snapped Lettie. "Well, if I were you, I shouldn't unpack my trunks just yet. I'm going to have a talk with Mrs. Crandall. Come along, Ina."

Thereupon she swept majestically out of the room, followed by Ina Mason.

Jean chuckled.

"We've made an enemy. She will never forgive us."

This was true. Lettie Briggs spent half an hour reminding Mrs. Crandall that her father was worth ten million dollars, but even so she did not get the study. She was furious, and unfortunately was the sort of girl who could nurse a grudge for a long time.

CHAPTER VIII

The Substitute Lamp

Doris Harland and Margaret Glenn dropped in to see the Dana girls that night and were warm in their admiration of the new study and its adjoining bedroom. Jean and Louise had lost no time in getting settled. They had unpacked their trunks, and the presence of their own belongings gave the place a comfortable and homelike air it had lacked earlier in the day.

"It's a sweet place," said Doris as she curled up on the window seat. "All the girls are envying you."

"Lettie Briggs decided to take it just as we were moving in," said Louise. "She was wild when we told her we had been assigned to it."

Doris sniffed. "I suppose her shadow was trailing along, too?"

"Ina? Oh, yes. They were just deciding where to hang their pennants when we marched in."

"I'm glad you got it," Margaret declared. "Lettie and Ina couldn't make the place look half so attractive and comfortable as you've made it."

Jean shook her head dubiously in reply.

"It's all right," she said, "but we're not satisfied yet. We need one thing more."

"A study lamp!" said Louise.

"Yes, it would be an improvement," the others admitted. "It's too bad your uncle's present was stolen."

"We intend to go shopping tomorrow and find a lamp to replace it. By the way," said Louise, "I haven't seen Evelyn Starr yet. Is she here?"

"The poor girl!" exclaimed Doris sympathetically. "I hear she isn't coming back to Starhurst."

"Not coming back!"

"It's just a rumor, of course," continued Doris, "and I shouldn't want it repeated, but I heard that it is because of—well—money. She can't afford to return."

There was a chorus of genuine regret. Evelyn, though a frail and wistful girl, was a general favorite at Starhurst.

"We met her brother," ventured Jean. "He visited our place the night before we came away."

"Franklin Starr!" exclaimed Margaret with interest. "Oh, do tell us about him. I've been crazy to meet him. Evelyn has often talked about him. He's a mysterious sort of man, isn't he? Always travelling. I know he has never visited Evelyn at the school."

The Dana girls explained how they had met Franklin Starr, although they modestly hurried over the details of the rescue at Oak Falls. They agreed with Margaret that the young man was indeed mysterious, having in mind his odd conduct and sudden departure after his overnight stay.

A little incident occurred when Margaret and Doris were leaving that evening. It seemed of slight significance at the time, but it was to have an important bearing on the subsequent adventures of the Dana girls at Starhurst. They were standing in the hall outside their door saying good-night to their visitors, when Jean ran her hand casually over a quaintly carved newel post at the foot of the stairs leading to the upper floor. To her surprise, the top of the post turned suddenly in her hand.

It was not, as she had supposed, part of the solid post. The ornamental top had simply been screwed on. The other girls did not notice the incident and Jean thought little of it, as she screwed the top tightly back into place.

"Queer," she said to herself. "I always supposed those posts were made all in one piece."

When they returned to their study, Louise looked around the comfortable old room. It lacked, as Jean had said, but one thing. A study lamp.

"We'll make the rounds of the stores tomorrow," she said. "We ought to be able to pick up a good lamp very cheap."

"Especially if we try the secondhand shops," remarked Jean.

On the following afternoon they went into Penfield to look for something suitable. They did not go to the big stores, acting on Jean's suggestion that they might find a bargain in the secondhand shops. After visiting several of these places, however, they were still empty-handed.

"After seeing that beautiful lamp Uncle Ned gave us," sighed Louise, "I hardly think I could ever be satisfied with any other."

Suddenly Jean halted with a cry of delight. "Louise! Look!"

There in a shabby window stood a lamp that was an exact duplicate of their present from Uncle Ned. They were so astonished that for a moment they could only stare at the gorgeous piece beyond the glass.

"Why—one might think," stammered Louise, "that it was the lamp which was stolen from us!"

"Quick!" said Jean, dragging her sister into the shop. "Somebody may buy it while we stand here gaping."

The proprietor of the shop, an elderly, near-sighted man, smiled when the girls inquired about the lamp. He recognized them as being from Starhurst.

"Yes," he chuckled, "that antique is a beauty. It has attracted a lot of attention—and I just put it in the window this morning. I got it in a shipment of goods. One of my dealers picked it up."

"Do you know where he got it?" asked Louise suddenly, as the thought came to her that it might be the same lamp that had been stolen. The man's next words contradicted that supposition.

"Gentleman going to Europe was selling all his effects," he said, taking the prize out of the window. "There you are, young ladies, and it's a bargain. You may have it for fifty dollars, no more, no less, and it's worth more than twice that."

"It really is a bargain," they agreed.

"Two young ladies from Starhurst were looking at it this morning, but they couldn't make up their minds. Wanted me to let them have it for forty dollars. If you really want the lamp, I'd advise you to buy it now, for I imagine they'll be back when they see they can't beat me down."

Louise took fifty dollars from her purse. "We'll take it," she said quickly.

The shopkeeper wrapped up the package. The girls were delighted with their purchase, for it seemed a rare piece of good luck that they had been able to find a lamp so closely duplicating the one they had lost. They were just about to leave the store when the door opened and two girls came in.

They were Lettie Briggs and Ina Mason. Lettie sauntered in with a bored expression on her pinched, disagreeable face. Ina, looking more like a very meek and unobtrusive shadow than ever, trailed at her heels.

"Hello, girls!" greeted Jean cheerfully. "Doing your Christmas shopping early?"

Lettie looked somewhat taken aback.

"I don't do my Christmas shopping in secondhand stores," she returned loftily. She brushed past the Dana girls and spoke to the proprietor.

"I think fifty dollars is a perfectly exorbitant price to pay for that lamp," she said.

"I don't think so, Miss. It was a real bargain," he answered.

Lettie did not realize the significance of the word "was." It was well-known at Starhurst that the spoiled girl, in spite of her big allowance, was very mean and haggled over every purchase.

"I'll give you forty-five dollars for it."

The man smiled.

"No, Miss," he said quietly, "you won't get the lamp for forty-five dollars."

"Very well, then," snapped Lettie. "Fifty dollars, but it's an outrage. It's sheer robbery."

"I wouldn't rob you, Miss," he returned,

evidently enjoying himself. "You won't get the lamp for fifty dollars or sixty dollars or eighty dollars or a hundred dollars. It's sold."

"Sold!" exploded Lettie. "But I told you— why, I practically bought that lamp—I had my heart set on it—why, you might have known——"

"You had your heart set on it at your own price," said the dealer, "but you missed your chance. I have just sold the lamp to these young ladies for fifty dollars."

Lettie whirled around and glared at the Dana girls.

"That lamp is mine!" she stormed. "How dared you buy it? Why, I made up my mind that I wanted it the moment I saw it. You have no right to buy it."

"We made up our minds the moment we saw it, too," replied Jean sweetly. "It was just the sort of piece we were looking for. Sorry, Lettie, but we didn't object to paying fifty dollars for it and now it's ours."

It would be a reflection on the standards of Starhurst School to say that Lettie Briggs raved, but her voice did rise to a most unladylike screech as she insisted upon what she called her rights. The Dana girls, however, were firm and finally departed from the store in triumphant possession, leaving the crestfallen Lettie explaining to Ina that she "never did like that pair of upstarts and never would."

On their return to the school they were passing the open door of the office when they noticed a slender, shabbily dressed girl sitting in front of Mrs. Crandall's desk. The principal was talking earnestly to her.

"Why, it's Evelyn Starr!" gasped Louise.

Evelyn's presence in Mrs. Crandall's office could mean but one thing—that she was returning to Starhurst. The girls were delighted, for they had been sorry to hear that financial difficulties might prevent her return. As they passed the doorway, they heard Evelyn's voice.

"I promise you faithfully, Mrs. Crandall, that the money will be paid during the semester. My brother has done the best he can and I do want to finish my course, but I can't pay tuition fees just now——"

The girls hurried on. They had not been able to help overhearing the proud but wistful voice.

"Then it must be true," whispered Jean.

"Poor Evelyn. It must be terrible for her. And to think that this whole place was once her home!"

Their knowledge of Evelyn Starr's misfortunes for a time overshadowed their delight in the new lamp.

"I'm not surprised Franklin Starr acted strangely," said Jean, as they reached their study. Her pretty face, framed in its halo of blonde hair, was serious. "He is probably half insane with worry. When people have had a great deal of money, I imagine they find it more difficult to face poverty than those who are used to being poor.''

''We'll have to do our best to see she has a good time while she's at Starhurst,'' declared the practical Louise. ''We can help a little that way.''

The lamp was duly connected and switched on. It cast a soft rosy glow that suddenly made the big room seem twice as warm and cozy, leaving mellow shadows in the corners, and softening every outline that had seemed harsh and hard in the early October twilight.

''Why, it's even more beautiful than I thought it would be!'' exclaimed Jean.

At that moment they heard a startled voice from the doorway.

''Where, oh where did you get that beautiful lamp? I'd recognize it anywhere!''

In the doorway stood Evelyn Starr.

CHAPTER IX

FAY VIOLETTE

"COME in, Evelyn!" cried Louise. "We're so glad to see you at Starhurst again."

"I arrived only an hour ago," said Evelyn. She spoke in an abstracted manner and seemed unable to take her eyes from the new table ornament.

"I happened to glance in as I was passing your door," she explained, "and when I saw that lamp I was so surprised—I—I really couldn't help speaking. I've seen it before, you know."

"Sit down and tell us about it," invited Jean, bringing Evelyn over to the window seat. "We have a great deal to tell you, too."

"It's very strange," said Evelyn. "I can't understand it. Years ago, I can remember that very lamp, standing right where it is now, in this very room."

"The same lamp!" exclaimed Louise. "Are you sure? We bought it in a secondhand shop a little while ago."

Evelyn went over to the beautiful object on the table and examined it closely.

"I'm quite sure," she said thoughtfully. "If it isn't the same one, it is a very clever imitation of the original. For *ours* was the original."

"It belonged to your father?"

Evelyn nodded.

"When we lived here at Starhurst, the lamp was sent to my father by a friend in Italy. And now it is back again."

The Dana girls were struck by the remarkable coincidence. They told Evelyn about the theft of the present given them by Uncle Ned and explained how they had seen the duplicate in the window of the Penfield store. In the course of their story Jean mentioned the name of Franklin Starr.

"You know my brother?" asked Evelyn in surprise.

"And *that*," declared Louise, "is another story. Indeed, we do know him. He stayed over night at our home just before we came to Starhurst——"

At that moment there was an interruption, as a freshman put her head in at the door.

"Dana girls wanted in the office," she sang out and fled.

The sisters were surprised. A summons to the office was unusual.

"We haven't had time to get into any mischief yet," said Jean, wrinkling her brow. "I can't imagine why we're wanted."

"Unless Lettie Briggs has appealed to Mrs. Crandall to make us sell her the lamp," laughed Louise. "You'll wait, won't you, Evelyn?"

The sisters hurried off downstairs. Quietly entering Mrs. Crandall's office, they found the headmistress of Starhurst in conversation with a visitor, a middle-aged woman whom they recognized instantly as Mrs. Grantland, the lady whose suitcase they had recovered at Penfield station.

"Are these the girls who were with you on the train, Mrs. Grantland?" asked Mrs. Crandall.

"Yes. They saw that fortune teller going away with my suitcase. I'm sure they didn't have anything to do with the loss of my ring— and yet I was so flustered and excited——"

"Girls," said Mrs. Crandall, "I have called you here to ask you a few questions. Mrs. Grantland tells me you were on the same train on which she came to Penfield yesterday."

"We remember Mrs. Grantland very well," said Louise. "Has she lost something?"

"I have lost a ring," announced Mrs. Grantland. "It was a pearl ring and very valuable. I was wearing it when I boarded the train, but after I reached Penfield it was missing."

Her manner was nervous and excited. It was plain that she was deeply worried over the loss of her piece of jewelry.

"I—I wondered," she faltered, "if any of

you girls—if you might have found it on the train.''

Jean shook her head.

''If we had found it,'' she said with dignity, ''we should have tried to find the owner.''

''Oh, I'm sure of that!'' declared the woman apologetically. ''I didn't mean—I don't insinuate that anyone stole it.''

Jean suddenly remembered the little episode on the train when the gypsylike woman was telling Mrs. Grantland's fortune.

''Perhaps I have no right to say it,'' she returned, ''but don't you think it was a bit unwise to have your fortune told by that stranger? The woman who looked like a gypsy? I have often heard that such people are apt to rob their patrons when they are pretending to be reading their palms. After all, she did try to walk away with your suitcase.''

''Do you know the woman's name?'' asked Mrs. Crandall sharply.

''She got on the train at Oak Falls,'' replied Louise. ''We saw her in a secondhand shop the day before we left. But we don't know her name.''

''That woman stole my ring!'' declared Mrs. Grantland positively. ''Oh, I'm sure of it. I remember now, she held my fingers very tightly when she was reading my hand. She might have slipped the ring off, and I wouldn't have noticed it. I was absorbed in what she

was telling me about having so much good luck."

"She seems to have contradicted herself," observed Mrs. Crandall, dryly.

"Oh, what shall I do?" exclaimed Mrs. Grantland, who seemed to be a good-natured but rather helpless individual. "I must have my ring! It's worth more than a thousand dollars. I'm nearly distracted."

"I'm afraid you won't find your jewelry unless you find that fortune teller," said Mrs. Crandall.

"We'll be on the watch for her," promised Jan.

Although the Dana girls were sympathetic, they realized that they could not be of much aid, however, unless they happened to see the gypsylike woman again.

"Thank you," returned Mrs. Grantland. "If you could only learn her name or find out where she lives! But I'm afraid my ring is gone. I shall never see it again."

Despite the fact that the girls had little hope of encountering the mind reader, they were destined to hear of her again before twenty-four hours had passed. And the study lamp, which seemed to be in the background of so many odd episodes, was again responsible.

They were in Penfield after classes the following afternoon, walking past the secondhand shop where they had bought the lamp, when

they heard a sharp tap on the window. Looking up, Jean saw the storekeeper beckoning to them.

"I don't suppose you young ladies would care to sell the lamp you bought from me yesterday?" he inquired.

"Sell the lamp!" exclaimed Louise.

"Not at the same price, of course," said the man hastily. "I can promise you a nice little profit on the deal if you care to part with your purchase."

"We wouldn't think of selling it," Louise told him promptly. "It was just the lamp we wanted."

"Why do you wish to buy it back?" asked Jean. Her first suspicion was that Lettie Briggs had asked the dealer to make the offer.

"You will remember that the antique came to me among the effects of a man who is leaving for Europe. I didn't arrange the deal myself, but the articles were offered to me by a woman—a Miss Fay Violette. Now, Miss Violette came into the store last night and explained that the lamp had been included in the property by mistake. She would like to have it back. She tells me that she really had no right to sell the piece at all, but of course she is willing to pay a little extra for its return."

"Would you mind describing Miss Violette?" asked Louise quickly. "Does she look like a gypsy?"

"Well, now that you come to mention it, she does," returned the man. "She has very dark eyes——"

"—and wears a great many rings and beads," added Jean.

"Do you know Miss Violette?" exclaimed the dealer in surprise.

"I believe we have met her," Louise said. "But I hardly think we care to sell the lamp—not even to Fay Violette."

"She said she wouldn't mind paying seventy dollars to get it back," urged the dealer.

Louise had her own ideas about the affair. She was beginning to wonder if their purchase was not, after all, the original lamp that had been stolen from them and not a duplicate. It seemed probable that the Fay Violette who had sold the object to the dealer was the cruel-eyed woman of Jake Garbone's secondhand shop. The story that the antique was among the effects of "a gentleman going to Europe" might be sheer fiction.

"If she really wants the lamp, she had better see us," said Louise firmly.

"Very well," replied the dealer. "I can't say I blame you for not wanting to sell it back. After all, you bought it in good faith and you have a right to keep it if you wish."

When they left the store, Louise voiced her suspicions to Jean.

"Do you know," she said, "I really believe

we've bought our own gift! Jake Garbone stole it, and when he knew he was suspected, he gave it to that woman to sell for him. She came to Penfield with it.''

"But why does she want it back?"

"That's what I can't understand."

"We're not going to part with it," declared Jean. "We bought it and we're going to keep it, whether it's the original lamp or not. There's something strange about the whole business."

"We know the woman's name, at any rate. We can tell Mrs. Grantland. Perhaps she'll be able to get her ring back."

The sisters returned to Starhurst. When they entered their study, they found that some mail, delivered in their absence, was lying on the table. There was a letter addressed in Uncle Ned's handwriting, a weirdly scrawled envelope that could have been sent by no one else than "Applecore," and a third letter smelling of cheap perfume, with the address written in purple ink on pink paper.

"I don't recognize this stationery," said Jean, as she tore open the envelope. "I smell a mystery."

Before reading the message, Jean glanced first at the signature.

"Why, it's from Fay Violette!" she exclaimed.

CHAPTER X

THE INQUISITIVE PLUMBER

THE letter, which was addressed to "The Miss Danas, Starhurst School," was brief. It read:

"Dear Miss Danas: I am told that you bot a lamp wich I sold by mistak and I want to buy it back if you will come to the Penfield House with the lamp I will pay you well for it. I will be at the Penfield House tomorro afternoon and I hope you will come with the lamp.

Yours respect'ly,
FAY VIOLETTE."

"She *is* determined!" Louise exclaimed. "Shall we go?"

"With the lamp? Certainly not. I think she is very impudent. The thing is probably ours in the first place. If it is, she most likely knows who stole it. Whether it is the original or not, we paid fifty dollars for it and I think we have a right to keep our purchase."

"I was thinking," said Jean slowly, "that

we should let Mrs. Grantland know about this. It would be a good chance for her to question the woman about her ring.''

''We'll tell Mrs. Crandall.''

''We'll have to tell her in any case, for the Penfield House is out of bounds. It's a cheap, shabby little hotel up in the north end of the town, and we'll have to get permission to go there.''

Louise decided to explain the situation to the principal at once and hurried off with the note. Jean switched on the study lamp, drew a chair up to the desk, and settled down to work at her algebra.

She was deep in the adventures of the famous x and his inseparable companion y who were engaged in a walking contest which was more perplexing than their usual activities, when she heard a gentle tap in the hall.

Looking up, she saw a man standing in the open doorway of the room. He was in overalls, wore spectacles and a small but ambitious mustache, and looked timid and inoffensive. He carried a monkey wrench.

''Yes?'' said Jean.

''Pardon, Miss,'' he said, ''but I'm one of the plumbers. We're trying to trace a leak in the water system. Do you mind if I look at the hot water pipes?''

''Not at all,'' Jean assured him, and resumed her studies.

The man came quietly into the room. She heard him tapping the pipes industriously, while a housemaid was busy near by dusting the hallway. After a while the work ceased. Jean glanced over the top of her book and was surprised to see that the plumber was staring intently at the study lamp.

He did not notice that he was observed. For nearly a minute he gazed at the object, a strange expression on his face. Then he caught Jean's curious look, started hastily, and bent over the pipes again. A few minutes later he quietly left the room.

Jean was puzzled by the plumber's apparent interest in the lamp, but the problems of x and y again engaged her attention and the incident slipped from her mind. Louise returned a few minutes later to say that Mrs. Crandall had given permission for the visit to Fay Violette the following afternoon.

"She telephoned to Mrs. Grantland, and that lady wants to come with us."

"I'm afraid she'll be disappointed if she hopes to get her ring again," said Jean. "After all, she has no proof that Fay Violette stole it, has she?"

"Perhaps something will come of the visit, anyway. I'm eager to learn more about that fortune teller."

Jean had forgotten the incident of the plumber. Had she mentioned it, Louise might have been more impressed by a little episode that occurred the following morning. The investigations of the plumbers had evidently failed to solve the problem of the water leak, for the men were back at Starhurst early the next day, prowling about the cellars and industriously examining pipes in the rooms and corridors. Louise was hurrying back to the study after morning classes when she saw a man in the hall just outside the Dana girls' room.

He was not aware of her approach. He had discovered the loose newel post on the stairs, had unscrewed it, and was gazing earnestly into the hole.

"Queer place to look for defective plumbing," thought Louise, as she hurried by.

Had Louise mentioned the incident to Jean, she would have heard the story of the inquisitive artisan who had been so deeply interested in the study lamp, for he was the same man— quiet, unobtrusive, bespectacled.

However, all thought of the plumber was driven from her mind when she entered the study to find Evelyn Starr huddled on the window seat, sobbing, her face hidden in the cushions.

"Why, Evelyn!" cried Louise. "What's the matter?"

The weeping girl sat up quickly and brushed the tears from her eyes. She tried to pretend

that she had not been crying, but the attempt
was a failure, for her lips quivered and her
cheeks were tear-stained.

Louise put her arm about the girl's shoul=
ders.

"What is the trouble, my dear?"

"N-nothing."

"But there *is* something and you must tell
me. Can I help?"

"You are so sweet to me," Evelyn sobbed,
"but I must not bother you with my worries."

As she hesitated, Louise asked, "Have you
had some disturbing news from your brother?"

"Yes, yes," cried Evelyn, burying her head
on her friend's shoulder, and ready now to
ask for sympathy. "I have had a terrible
shock. I am afraid something dreadful is going to happen to Franklin."

As the girl paused again, Louise prompted
her to unburden her troubles, by inquiring how
she had heard this distressing news.

From her blouse Evelyn produced a
crumpled letter, and opening it with trembling
fingers, she read in a broken voice:

"'My dear Sister Evelyn: I am not
staying in the town where I am mailing this
letter, so do not try to find me. I am
sending to you all the money I have in the
world. My head hurts so much at this moment that I am afraid of myself——' "

She could read no further, and thrust the
letter into Louise's hand, saying, "You may
finish it."

The Dana girl caught her breath as she
perused the incoherent and heart-rending sen-
tences from this brother who, she guessed, was
in such great difficulties both financially and
physically, yet was using all his strength to
take care of the young sister he adored.

Louise did her best to comfort her unhappy
schoolmate, trying to assure her that everything
would come out all right in a short time.

"I really shouldn't be at Starhurst at all,"
cried the distracted girl, "because I know my
brother needs this money as much as I do. And
to think I do not know where he is, so that I
can go to him and give it back."

"He wants you to stay at school," Louise
reminded her. "He realizes that under the
conditions this is the best place for you to be."

"But," objected Evelyn, "this amount of
money will not keep me here very long, and
then I shall have to go away, anyhow. But
that is not what worries me most. I want to
find my brother and help him if he is in
trouble."

After several minutes Louise succeeded in
quieting her friend, and even got her to promise
that she would try to be brave. To herself
Louise resolved that she, with Jean's help,
would try to locate the missing Franklin Starr.

"You see," Evelyn said at last, "I can't get used to the idea of not having any money. When we lived at Starhurst, I had everything I needed. This room was beautiful. It was our library, and the lamp is like the one we owned, and I loved it so much."

As she said these words, she ran her frail fingers lovingly over the base of the electric ornament. Evelyn turned to leave the room. She smiled at Louise.

"I cannot think of any girls I should rather see have a lamp like this than you and Jean. You have been wonderful friends to me, and I shall never forget your sympathy."

As Evelyn softly closed the study door, Louise could not help but admire the girl's courage. At the same time she hoped fervently that Franklin Starr would soon overcome his financial difficulties, for Evelyn's sake at least.

Jean came in a few minutes later and put her schoolbooks on the table.

"Mrs. Crandall just stopped me in the hall to say that Mrs. Grantland would call for us after luncheon. And Louise, she's bringing a detective with her."

"A detective!" exclaimed Louise. "Why?"

"Perhaps she hopes he'll be able to trick Fay Violette into a confession. At any rate," concluded Jean, "our little visit promises to be interesting."

CHAPTER XI

A Strange Interview

The Penfield House was not the leading hotel of the town. On the contrary, it was Penfield's cheapest and shabbiest hostelry, an old frame building that was more like a second-rate boarding house than an hotel. Even in the company of the detective, Mrs. Grantland said she was nervous on entering it, for the reputation of the place was not of the best.

The detective was a tall, thin man by the name of Sedgwick. He had promised to do what he could toward recovering Mrs. Grantland's pearl ring, but he admitted that he had very little hope of success.

"You aren't sure she took it," he pointed out, "and naturally she'll deny stealing it. However, I'll do my best. We'll let these young ladies go ahead first and have their interview with the woman. If we all go in together, she'll blame them for putting me on her trail."

"Perhaps that will be wise," agreed Mrs. Grantland. "I don't want to make trouble for the girls, of course."

So, while Mrs. Grantland and the detective

waited in a small office on the ground floor of the hotel, Jean and Louise went up to a little parlor where they came face to face with Fay Violette.

She looked more like a gypsy than ever, although the Danas were positive she was not of Romany extraction. Her white, sinister face was framed by a colorful shawl flung over her head and drawn together at her throat by a huge brooch. There were bracelets and bangles on her wrists, rings on her fingers, heavy strings of beads about her neck.

Her presence in the hotel was explained by a large poster tacked to the wall. It depicted a human hand, the lines of which were identified in heavy print as "Life Line," "Heart Line," and similar terms of palmistry. Fay Violette had set up as a fortune teller.

"You are the Dana girls?" she asked eagerly as they came into the room.

"Yes," said Louise, "but we came to tell you that we couldn't possibly consider selling the lamp."

A dangerous light flashed in the woman's eyes for a moment, then it was gone. With no hint of anger in her voice, she replied:

"But it means so much to me, and it is only an old lamp. I would pay you well."

"It happens to be an exact duplicate of one that was stolen from us a few days ago," said Louise. "In fact," she continued, with a shrewd glance at Fay Violette, "it might even be the same lamp. We couldn't think of parting with it."

"I sold it to the dealer," said Fay Violette, "when I had no right to do so. It was a mistake. It means a great deal of trouble for me unless I bring it back."

"Where did you get it?" asked Jean.

"A gentleman who is going to Europe asked me to get rid of some of his goods," returned the woman smoothly. "After I had taken them away, he asked me about the lamp. He told me that piece was not to be sold. But, by that time——"

She shrugged.

"That's too bad," said Louise, "but it really isn't our fault."

"Then you will not sell the lamp? It means so much trouble for me."

"Is it very valuable?" asked Jean. "Is that why the man wants it back? Because it is worth much more than we paid for it?"

"No. Oh, no," said Fay Violette hastily— too hastily. "He wants it because it has been in his family for a long time."

"As a matter of fact," said Louise, who did not believe a word of this story, "we think it is the same lamp that was stolen from us."

"Impossible," said Fay Violette. "There must be two alike."

"Perhaps."

The woman pleaded with them, but the Dana girls remained firm. They were positive that their gift had been stolen by Jake Garbone, and that he had commissioned Fay Violette to sell it for him. Now, for some mysterious reason, he wanted it back.

"I'll give you seventy dollars for it," offered the fortune teller.

"It isn't a matter of money," Louise told her. "We simply want to keep the lamp."

"Eighty dollars—ninety-five!"

Still they refused.

"A hundred and fifty dollars. Come! That is three times what you paid for it."

"We wouldn't sell it for two hundred dollars," declared Jean.

"Two hundred dollars is a great deal of money for a lamp. You are bargaining with me. You know I *must* have it. Very well, two hundred dollars."

"I said we *wouldn't* sell it for two hundred dollars."

"Not for five hundred," said Louise.

Fay Violette was crestfallen. She bit her lip. She disguised her wrath, however, and pretended to dismiss the matter.

"If you will not sell, I suppose I must explain it to the owner somehow," she sighed.

"We are the owners now."

"By accident," returned the woman, with a trace of bitterness in her voice. Suddenly she reached forward and took Jean's hand. "Come, we will forget about the lamp. I shall argue no more. You must let me read your palm."

"I don't believe in fortune telling," said Jean nervously.

"You must not say that. Everything is written in the hand. Your whole life is written there if one can but read it. See! This little line. It means trouble. Trouble for you before long. And this line—it tells of the past. I see a thief. He is very close to you. In your house. You have done him a great favor. You have saved his life."

The girls were surprised. She could mean only one man. Franklin Starr.

"There is a dog. The thief owns a dog. I see a river, too. There is danger. You save this man from danger in the river. But he is a thief. He steals something you value a great deal."

"How can you tell all that from my palm?" asked Jean incredulously.

"It is written. Everything is written," droned the woman. "I can read the past, the present, and the future. I see trouble for you in the future. You will meet this thief again. You must be on your guard against him. He will come as a friend, but you must not trust him too much."

Suddenly she relinquished Jean's hand.

"I can tell you more," she said in a very

businesslike tone, "if you will cross my palm with silver."

But Jean shook her head.

"I don't believe in fortune telling."

"Have I not told you the truth? Did you not remember the man with the dog? Did you not save his life from the river?"

"I don't know how you learned that, but I'm sure it wasn't in my palm."

"Come, Jean," said Louise, who was deeply puzzled by the woman's evident knowledge of the affair of Franklin Starr, "we'll have to go."

"And you won't sell that lamp?" asked Fay.

"I'm sorry," Louise answered. "We don't care to part with it."

Fay Violette gave no sign of the fact that she was furious with the girls.

"There is bad luck attached to that lamp," she said slowly. "The owner told me that it brought misfortune to everyone but him. It always comes back to him."

"We'll take our chance on the bad luck," returned Jean lightly.

They went downstairs where they rejoined Mrs. Grantland and the detective.

"Now," said Mr. Sedgwick, "we'll go up and see what we can do about that pearl ring. If she's as smart as I think she is, we won't get it."

The man was right. When he came back with Mrs. Grantland fifteen minutes later, he shook

his head mournfully. His companion looked
distressed.

"I knew it," said the detective. "She denies
up and down that she took the ring. She knows
we can't prove anything."

"And I'm positive that she stole it from me,"
declared Mrs. Grantland, her voice trembling.
"She's perfectly brazen. She admits she told
my fortune on the train. She admits I was
wearing the ring. She even tried to hint that
some of the schoolgirls might have taken it."

"I knew we wouldn't get anywhere," said
Sedgwick, who was a very discouraging sort
of detective indeed. "You must have proof.
That's what counts. But we'll trap her. She
won't keep that ring. She'll try to sell it, if
she hasn't sold it already. It may turn up, and
if it does, we'll trace the person who sold it.
And that person, if I'm not greatly mistaken,
will be Miss Fay Violette."

They went away from the hotel. Mrs. Grantland, although disappointed at the outcome of
her visit, thanked the girls warmly for their
help.

"It was very good of you to come with me,"
she told them. "I appreciate it very much."

She drove them back to Starhurst in her car.
When the girls were back in their study again,
Jean said:

"I don't believe in fortune telling, Louise,
but it *was* strange how that woman described

Franklin Starr. Do you think he could have taken the lamp?"

"I don't believe he is a thief, whatever Fay Violette may say. It is odd, though, that she knew we had rescued him at Oak Falls."

"She heard about that affair, somehow. She couldn't read it in my palm," declared Jean.

"I know one person who would believe every word of it," laughed Louise.

"Who is that?"

" 'Applecore.' "

"Poor Applecore. Seven years of bad luck. And Fay Violette said she saw trouble in my hand. Applecore would say it was all coming true."

One remark made by the gypsy woman, however, stayed in Louise's mind. It was her statement that the lamp always brought bad luck to anyone save the original owner, and that the antique would always return to him eventually. She recalled the statement to Jean.

"She was trying to frighten us," declared Jean.

"I'd like to know," said Louise thoughtfully, "why she is so insistent upon having it back. If the dealer made a profit on it when he sold it to us for fifty dollars, he must have bought it from her for less."

"And yet she offered us two hundred dollars!"

There seemed to be no logical explanation of the lamp's sudden increase in value.

CHAPTER XII

The Plumber Again

EVELYN STARR and the Dana girls had become fast friends. During the previous semester at Starhurst the sisters had not been on intimate terms with the shy, reserved girl, but now the three were often together. Realizing that their friend was troubled and worried, the girls made it a point of inviting her frequently to their study and doing everything they could to make her forget her difficulties.

Evelyn appreciated their friendship. She had never been unpopular at Starhurst, but her bashfulness had prevented her from making any close chums. She was loyal and warmhearted, however, and in a short time Jean and Louise realized that she was a friend worth having.

Although Louise's sympathy and Jean's light-hearted gaiety dispelled some of the clouds of worry that hung over the girl, Evelyn was still troubled. The girls noticed that whenever the mail arrived at Starhurst, Evelyn scanned the letter rack with anxiety. She always turned away disappointed, her lips trembling. One morning she did receive a letter, tore it open quickly, and read it at a glance.

"I just knew there was something seriously wrong," she said to Louise. "Look at that."

The elder Dana girl took the letter. It was typewritten, and the signature was that of a legal firm in a near-by city.

The message was as follows:

"Dear Miss Starr: We are writing to ask if you have any information as to the whereabouts of your brother, Mr. Franklin Starr. He was to have kept a business appointment at this office some time ago, but he has not yet appeared. We have made every effort to get in touch with him, but he is not at his home address and we are unable to locate him. There are certain matters demanding adjustment, and we are eager to see him at the earliest opportunity. Please let us know if you have heard from your brother recently.

Faithfully yours,
ANDERS AND WOODS."

"It's very strange," agreed Louise. "Perhaps he really is in trouble."

"I'm dreadfully worried," said Evelyn. "In his last letter, you remember, he complained of having violent headaches. Oh, I do hope nothing has happened to him."

Jean and Louise remembered that Franklin Starr had complained of pains in his head when he was in Oak Falls, and wondered if he had injured his brain when he was knocked unconscious by his fall into the river.

"He may even have lost his memory and wandered away," said Evelyn anxiously. "I have read of such things. It is all so strange."

Jean and Louise did their best to comfort the uneasy girl. It was unusual, they agreed, that the lawyer had been unable to locate Franklin Starr, yet that did not necessarily mean that some mishap had befallen him.

"He might have been called away suddenly on business," argued Jean. "Keep up your courage, Evelyn. You may hear from him to-morrow."

Louise opened a letter that had come for the Dana girls in the same mail. From the folds of the heavy, expensive stationery dropped two theatre tickets.

"Oh, good!" cried Jean, picking up the bits of cardboard. "Who is being generous? Tickets to a show! Whom is the letter from, Louise?"

"Mrs. Grantland!"

She read the brief note. Mrs. Grantland again expressed her thanks for the help the girls had given her in locating Fay Violette. As a token of her gratitude she was enclosing two tickets for a special matinée performance

of a comedy success that was playing at the
Penfield Theatre during the current week.

"Isn't she a good soul!" exclaimed Louise,
highly delighted. "It seems ages since we've
seen a show."

"I've been hearing about that play for
months, but I never thought we'd be lucky
enough to see it. When do we go?"

Louise looked at the tickets.

"Why, the matinée is this afternoon!"

"This afternoon! Goodness, we'll have to
hurry. I'm glad we have no classes."

They dashed upstairs. When they entered
the study, their delight changed swiftly to
dismay.

The study lamp was gone!

"Someone has stolen it!" gasped Louise.
"It was here not ten minutes ago."

"Then it can't be far away. Let's get
busy."

They searched their rooms first, thinking that
some of the girls might have hidden the lamp
as a joke. But a diligent search failed to reveal the precious object.

"We'll have to do a little detective work,"
said Jean briskly.

"Do you think some of the workmen may
have taken it? They're still in the building."

"They wouldn't dare. But we'd better ask
the other girls. Someone may be able to give
us information."

They separated and visited various other rooms on the same floor of the building. No one, however, had seen anyone entering or leaving the Dana girls' study.

Jean went upstairs. Starhurst was a rambling old place, and besides the main staircases, there were several odd flights of steps joining the various floors. At a turn on one of these she suddenly blundered into a man.

It was the bespectacled plumber. With a chisel in his hand he was diligently prying at a panel in the old oak wall, trying to force it open. He had not been aware of Jean's approach and he turned quickly, as if startled.

"Pardon, Miss," he muttered as he stepped aside.

He thrust the tool into a pocket of his overalls and hastily descended the steps. There was a guilty, furtive air about him, suggesting that his activities were not wholly connected with the repairs to the water system.

"There's something strange about that man," thought Jean, as she went on to the upper floor. "I have an odd feeling that I've seen him somewhere else."

She could not recall any man, however, answering the description of the mysterious plumber.

It was from Doris Harland that she got her first clue about the missing lamp.

"Your lamp gone!" exclaimed Doris. "Isn't

that too bad? No, I haven't been downstairs
since morning classes—" Then, as a thought
suddenly struck her, she asked: "Have you
spoken to Lettie Briggs?"

"Why?"

"Well, I may be merely guessing, but it
strikes me that she and Ina have something up
their sleeves. They room next door to me, you
know, and they just came in a few minutes
ago. I've heard them laughing and giggling
ever since."

"Thanks," said Jean, and fled. Downstairs
she met Louise, to whom she told what Doris
had said.

"That pair may know something about it.
Let's go and ask them."

Louise frowned.

"One of the girls told me that Lettie and Ina
were down in the kitchen having a long talk
with the cook."

"That's suspicious. Lettie wouldn't set
foot in that place unless she had a very good
reason for it."

"I think we'd better see the cook first."

As the trail led to the kitchen, they set out
to interview Amanda, the colored cook. That
stout, jovial person was given to laughter and
the singing of hymns. Just now she was
chuckling placidly as she trimmed a pie crust.

"You seem happy, Amanda," said Jean.

"Lawsy, 'deed I is," beamed Amanda. looking up. "I'se jes' about the happies' woman around dis place, 'ceptin' nobody."

"Somebody must have left you a fortune." Amanda beamed.

"No, Miss. Nobody lef' me no fo'tune. No luck like dat for Amanda. But somebody done giv' me a *present!*"

"That's fine," declared Louise, as the solution of the mystery dawned on her. "Was it a lamp?"

Amanda gazed at her in astonishment.

"Now how did yo' all guess dat?" she exclaimed.

Jean put her arm around the cook's massive shoulders.

"I'm sorry we have to disappoint you, Amanda, but we have lost a lamp. Someone— er—borrowed it. For a joke, I suppose."

Amanda looked suddenly grim.

"De joke bein' on *me*, I s'pose. You jes' come along wid me and we's gwine find out if yo' lamp is my lamp. An' if it is, somebody is gwine stop laughin' mighty quick."

Amanda waddled away and disappeared into her room back of the kitchen. When she returned a few moments later, she was carrying the study lamp.

"Thought it seemed mighty funny dey should make such a fuss 'bout me for no reason 'tall and give me dat lamp 'cause dey like my cookin'."

"I'm sorry, Amanda. It *is* our lamp," said Louise.

The cook snorted and thrust the object into Jean's hands.

"Guess you was mighty worried, chile. I don' like dem kind of jokes. Not me. I'se no time to play jokes mahself."

So saying, she yanked open the door of a cupboard and took out a tray of crisp, tempting cream puffs. She offered one to each of the girls.

"Um!" said Jean. "You *do* know how to make cream puffs, Amanda."

"Dat's de troof!" declared Amanda. "But dey is cream puffs *and* cream puffs; an' I hopes dem bad girls gets none."

Then Jean had an idea while the cook resumed her work.

She delicately opened two of the cream puffs on the tray, seized a shaker of red pepper, and went to work. When she had finished, the pastry looked quite as succulent as ever, but the filling was entirely different.

"Now it's *my* turn to go around giving away presents," said Jean as she gathered up the two desserts. They hustled up the back stairs with the goodies and the lamp, after thanking Amanda for the treat.

"Jean," whispered Louise, who understood what her sister planned to do, "I do hope Lettie and Ina take a good big bite."

They met Evelyn Starr on the way. "Come on!" gasped Louise with suppressed laughter. "There's a little table-turning act due to start in about two minutes."

They reached Doris Harland's room by taking a short cut up the back stairs. In hurried whispers they explained the situation to her, and with stifled giggles the girls waited while Jean placed the puffs on a convenient window ledge down the hall near Lettie's room. Beyond the wall they could distinguish her occasional high-pitched laugh. She and her shadow were evidently enjoying their joke on the Dana girls. Lettie, however, stepped from her room before very long and espied the tempting pastry.

"Don't laugh, whatever you do," whispered Louise warningly, as she became aware of the actions of Lettie, "at least, not yet."

Jean promptly stuffed a handkerchief into her mouth.

Lettie's door closed again, and the listeners knew the dessert had been taken in to be eaten. Doris snickered. Jean fairly hugged herself in anticipation. They all sensed that soon there would be trouble down the corridor when the chums found out the dainties were not a present from Amanda in return for the lamp.

A moment later there was a squeal from the room, followed by a muffled howl.

"Help! My mouth is burning up!"

screeched Lettie. "Water! Ina—get some water!"

"I'm scorched. My tongue is burnt!" howled Ina.

Riotous confusion prevailed. The listeners could hear the two victims running about and bumping into each other, gasping and spluttering. Then the door crashed open and the pair raced toward the bathroom, there to soothe their burning mouths with cold water.

Jean burst into a peal of laughter. It was the signal for an outburst of uncontrollable mirth that brought girls flocking from their rooms. By the time the crestfallen Lettie emerged from the bathroom, followed by Ina Mason dutifully carrying a large jug of water, the joke was common property.

"One good turn deserves another, Lettie!"

The victim of the joke glared, tried to speak, and then choked again as a few stray grains of pepper manifested their presence. She flounced into her room. Ina Mason barely sidled over the threshold before the door slammed.

The sisters and Evelyn returned to the Dana study, pleased with the outcome of their joke.

"Perhaps we'd better lock our room before we go to the matinée," suggested Louise.

"It wouldn't be a bad idea," agreed Jean. "That joke gave me a scare. We might really lose the lamp."

"You shouldn't have to lock your study,"
said Evelyn Starr. "Let me guard the lamp
while you're gone. I'll bring my books down
and work here."

The girls accepted their friend's offer with
relief.

"To tell you the truth," said Louise, while
she was getting dressed, "I don't trust some of
those workmen who have been around here.
There is one in particular I have in mind."

CHAPTER XIII

The Hidden Watcher

"Who is it that you don't trust?" asked Jean, as she pulled off her school frock and prepared to bathe before attending the matinée. "Oh, dear, I've torn the hem in my skirt. I'll bet I did that when I hurried up the back stairs with those cream puffs."

"It's a wonder you ever delivered them safely, you were running so fast," said Evelyn laughingly, meanwhile connecting up the lost lamp and adjusting it on the study table.

"What a job I did have to keep them right side up," returned Jean as she started toward the bathroom, throwing a gay kimono over her.

"But you didn't tell me who it was you don't trust, Louise."

"I mean the workman that wears glasses and has a small mustache."

"I'm suspicious of him, too!" exclaimed Jean. "When we were looking for the lamp, I came upon him on one of the stairways. He was prying at a wall panel with a chisel. When he saw me, he put the tool into his overall pocket and hurried out."

"Why," said Louise, "that's the man I saw. He was looking into one of the chest window seats. There are no water pipes in the window seats at Starhurst, not that I know of, at any rate."

"The workmen will be around for a few days, I hear," said Evelyn. "It seems that Mr. and Mrs. Crandall have decided to improve the east wing and have the rooms there redecorated. When we lived here, we had so many people working around, I didn't think a thing about it—they were all over."

"Well," laughed Jean, "if any one of them comes snooping around here while we're away, chase him out. Throw a book at him. Use my algebra, if you like. I'm often tempted to throw it out of the window myself."

The girls reached the theatre in good time. They had not looked closely at their tickets and were surprised when a respectful usher led them, not to gallery or orchestra seats, but to a box. A woman was already sitting there.

"Mrs. Grantland!" exclaimed Jean with pleasure. "How lovely of you to give us this treat."

"It's little enough, my dears," returned Mrs. Grantland, smiling. "I was very eager to see this play and it is more fun when one has company. I should have called for you, but I was busy until the last minute. Make yourselves comfortable."

In the unaccustomed luxury of a box seat the Dana girls enjoyed every moment of the afternoon. The play was clever and uproariously funny, the acting was good, and the whole performance was above the average. When it was over, they thanked their hostess warmly for her generosity.

"It was nothing," she said lightly.

"I don't suppose," ventured Louise, "that you have had any further news of your ring."

Mrs. Grantland shook her head.

"The detective has sent out a description of the ring, and I imagine the thief will have trouble trying to sell it without being caught. But that's small consolation. She may not try to sell it at all."

"You're convinced, then, that the thief is Fay Violette?"

"Convinced!" said Mrs. Grantland. "I'm absolutely positive."

She drove the girls back to the school gates in her car. It had been a dull, foggy day, and darkness had come early. Lights gleamed from the student rooms as Jean and Louise went up the walk toward the huge old mansion.

"Well, our lamp hasn't been stolen," said Jean. "I can see its rays shining."

"Evelyn is still on guard."

They could see the window of their study quite clearly. The lamp cast a circle of light onto the ground below. Suddenly into this circle stepped the figure of a man. He halted and stood looking upward.

The girls paused, wondering what this might mean.

"He's spying on our room!" declared Louise indignantly.

The stranger appeared to realize that he was conspicuous, for at that moment he withdrew slowly into the shadows of the trees near by. During his brief appearance the girls noticed that his coat collar was turned up about his ears and that his hat was drawn low on his forehead.

Jean was never timid.

"I'm going to ask him what he's up to," she announced flatly. "The idea! Mrs. Crandall would have him arrested if she knew."

Louise restrained her impetuous sister.

"If we walk right across to the window now, he'll see us. He'll be gone before we're half way across the lawn. Let's circle around and come up behind him. Somehow, Jean—he looked familiar."

"I had the same notion," Jean admitted.

"Franklin Starr!" whispered Louise.

"It couldn't be Franklin Starr. This man is of about the same height and build, and there was something about him that reminded me of Franklin Starr, but—oh, it's not possible. What would he be doing loitering around Starburst like this?" Meanwhile Jean and Louise sneaked up behind him and said) BOO! HA! HA!

"It's unlikely, I know. But let's slip over among the trees and come up behind him."

Cautiously the girls made their way across the gloomy lawn. The darkness and the heavy shadows of the trees afforded excellent cover. From time to time they could distinguish the stranger, standing just beyond the bright circle of light from the study window. Once they caught a glimpse of Evelyn's fair hair as she bent over her books at the desk.

Jean stepped on a twig and it snapped with a sharp noise. They saw the stranger turn and peer toward them through the gloom. Then, alarmed, he dashed off into the shadows. The girls broke into a run and gave chase, but in a few minutes they had lost their quarry in the darkness.

"He's gone!" said Jean, exasperated. "Let's go and tell Mrs. Crandall. She'll have the grounds searched."

Louise maintained that this was useless.

"He's probably out of this place by now. And, besides—he *did* remind me of Franklin Starr."

"But why would Franklin Starr, of all people, be eavesdropping here at Starhurst?"

"Why not?" argued Louise. "Perhaps his troubles have unbalanced his mind. Perhaps he has lost his memory. That would explain why the lawyers haven't been able to locate him. Starhurst was his old home, remember. If he *has* lost his memory, isn't it probable that he would instinctively drift back here?''

Her sister's reasoning appealed to Jean.

"There may be something in what you say," she admitted. "Do you think we should tell Evelyn?"

"I don't suppose it would do any harm. After all, it may help her believe he is at least alive. I know she has been worrying dreadfully. She is afraid he may have been killed."

When the girls returned to their study, they found Evelyn patiently working at her books. They told her about the stranger they had seen beneath the window and cautiously voiced their suspicions that the man might have been Franklin Starr.

"Of course we may be mistaken," said Jean, "but we were both struck by the resemblance. We weren't near enough to see his face."

They ventured the theory that Franklin Starr might be suffering from loss of memory or a nervous breakdown.

Evelyn was greatly upset.

"It's a big relief to know that he is alive," she said, with tears in her eyes, "but it's dreadful to think that he may be in trouble and that I can't help him. If he *is* alive I can't imagine why he hasn't written to me again."

"I wish we could do something," said Jean.

"We can," declared Louise practically. "Of course, we don't know whether this man was

Franklin Starr or not. If it *was* Franklin Starr, then he is somewhere in or around Penfield. We can look for him."

"But we can't go searching around hotels and places like that," objected Jean.

"Not ourselves, but we can organize some sort of a search."

"How?" asked Evelyn eagerly.

"Mrs. Grantland's detective! What's his name—Sedgwick. We'll ask him to help."

"That's a splendid idea!" exclaimed Evelyn impulsively. "Oh, if we could do that, we might find my brother. We'll give him a complete description of Franklin and ask him to make inquiries everywhere."

The girls decided upon an immediate plan of action. They drew up a description of Franklin Starr, a description so complete that Sedgwick would have no trouble recognizing the missing man should he meet him face to face, and prepared to ask Mrs. Grantland for the "loan" of her detective.

With these preparations Evelyn had to be content. She said little, but the Dana girls knew she was oppressed with worry.

With the recollection of that lurking figure in the shadows beneath the study window, they wondered if Franklin Starr had, indeed, become unbalanced or had lost his memory. Was he now wandering, helpless, near his old boyhood home, unaware even of his own name?

CHAPTER XIV

A MALICIOUS RUMOR

MRS. GRANTLAND consented readily to ask her detective to search for Franklin Starr. Inasmuch as he was being paid for his time in looking for the ring, she felt, he might as well try to accomplish two tasks at the same time.

"But frankly, girls," she told the sisters, "I hardly think he'll find either the man or the ring. I'm beginning to lose faith in Mr. Sedgwick."

However, if Mrs. Grantland was beginning to lose faith in Mr. Sedgwick, the same could not be said of the detective himself. Armed with the description of Franklin Starr, he set out with all confidence.

"Don't worry, ladies," he said grandly. "If he is in Penfield, I'll find him. If I have a specialty at all, that specialty is finding missing persons. Would you believe it—a man once asked me to find his long-lost brother! Missing for sixteen years. Last heard of in Montana. I found that brother. I found him in less than two weeks."

"Where was he?" asked Jean eagerly.

"Running a grocery store just across the street."

"What street?"

"The same street the first brother lived on. There they were, living right across from each other, and didn't know it. Missing brother had changed his name. Never recognized each other. Very odd, some of the cases we handle."

The girls agreed that the case of the missing brothers was very odd indeed, although they were too polite to say they did not believe a word of it. However, Mr. Sedgwick set out on his search with such tremendous confidence that they could not help but be hopeful.

Two days passed.

Mr. Sedgwick reported that he was making progress.

Another day went by.

Mr. Sedgwick reported that he had made remarkable progress up to the point of locating a man who answered every detail of the description with the minor exceptions that he was bald-headed, ten years older than Franklin Starr, and was a perfectly respectable automobile salesman by the name of Cooperthwaite. The detective admitted that he had checked up on all the local hotels, clubs, and boarding houses without success.

The workmen were still at Starhurst. Jean had encountered the bespectacled plumber in the corridors several times, and on no occasion did his work appear to have the remotest connection with the water system. He seemed to spend the greater part of his time wandering aimlessly about, gazing at the walls and ceilings. Remembering his suspicious conduct on two other occasions, Jean told herself that the man would bear watching.

Coming up from the dining hall at noon a few days after the experience with the stranger underneath the study window, Jean passed a group of workmen at lunch in the hall near the entrance to the east wing. She noted that the mysterious plumber was not with the others. On her way to her own room she heard a strange tapping from the floor above.

Jean listened for a moment, puzzled. Most of the girls, she knew, were still in the dining hall. The tapping continued. Then she heard a wrenching sound, as if a board had been removed.

"I think I'll look into this," she said to herself.

Creeping quietly up the stairs toward the floor above, she reached a point where she had a clear view of the corridor. As she paused, she could see a crouching figure only a few yards away.

The mysterious plumber was taking advantage of his lunch hour and the absence of the girls from the floor to engage in some peculiar activities of his own. He had loosened two of the floor boards and was looking beneath them. As Jean watched, she saw him shake his head in disappointment.

He replaced the boards, then nailed them back and turned his attention to the baseboard of the corridor. With a small hammer he made his way along the wall, tapping lightly and listening intently to every impact of the steel tool.

This odd performance went on for several minutes. The man had no idea that he was being watched. As for Jean, she was greatly perplexed. That the fellow's activities had no connection with the duties for which he had been engaged was quite clear.

Suddenly there came a burst of laughter from below, together with a clatter of shoes as some of the girls came up from the dining hall. Jean turned and began to descend the stairs. She had gone only a few steps, however, before she met Lettie Briggs and Ina returning to their room. They looked at her curiously and then, when the plumber appeared at the head of the stairway a moment later, Lettie Briggs looked significantly at her companion.

"Seems as if we've disturbed a quiet little meeting," she said audibly.

Jean flushed, but hurried on down to the study. The plumber hastily brushed past Lettie and Ina, looking confused and nervous.

When Jean returned to her room, she found her sister gathering up notebooks.

"Louise, I'm suspicious of that plumber!" she declared.

"The fellow with the spectacles?"

Jean nodded.

"Remember, I told you of seeing him try to pry open a wall panel the other day. Well, he's still snooping around. I can't imagine what he's looking for. Just now he was on the upper floor, tapping at the baseboard and actually tearing up the corridor."

"Perhaps he's a robber in disguise," Louise suggested.

"What could he steal at Starhurst? The Crandalls aren't wealthy. They have no jewels—nothing but a few heirlooms. If he is a thief, why should he go prowling about in broad daylight?"

"Perhaps," said Louise, "we should tell Mrs. Crandall."

"But what could we tell her? Simply that we saw one of the plumbers acting suspiciously. We haven't seen him steal anything. As far as we know, nothing *has* been stolen. If he is a thief, he has been around the school long enough to rob half the rooms at Starhurst."

The girls decided to say nothing about the man, but to keep an eye on him when occasion warranted. They were still puzzling over his behavior when they heard a group of girls chattering in the hall. High above the other voices they heard the shrill tones of Lettie Briggs;

"—and when we came up the stairs, down came Miss Jean Dana, if you please, looking as embarrassed as if she'd been caught robbing the pantry. Well, naturally, we wondered what she had been up to, and it wasn't long before we found out. For right at her heels came—of all people—*one of the plumbers!*"

"No!" gasped one of the girls.

"Yes," squealed Lettie. "The two of them had been having a confidential little chat up at the head of the stairs. He was working up there and I suppose she just couldn't keep away from him. She was blushing right to the roots of her hair, and as for *him*—why, he couldn't look us in the face."

Jean straightened up, her eyes flashing.

"No wonder!" she snapped.

"Shh!" cautioned Louise.

"Which plumber was it?" came another voice.

"The man with the little mustache and the spectacles," giggled Lettie. "Can you imagine?"

"I've seen her watching him several times while he has been working in the building," said Ina Mason. "It just came to me in a flash. Jean Dana is in love with that plumber!"

There was a peal of excited laughter from the group in the hall. Jean leaped for the door and would have rushed out into the hall to deny the malicious story then and there, but Louise restrained her.

"Don't pay any attention," she advised. "Lettie hasn't anything better to do. If you make a fuss, it will simply attract further notice; and if you ignore that sort of silly gossip, it will blow over in a few hours."

Jean took her sister's advice. She affected utter indifference to the ill-natured rumor that Lettie and Ina industriously circulated through the school within the next day or so. Most of the girls knew the wealthy student's spiteful nature only too well, and if she had hoped to embarrass Jean by her tale, she was disappointed.

The trifling incident, however, was soon forgotten by the Dana girls in the light of a new and startling development. Once again Jake Garbone, the secondhand dealer, crossed their path!

CHAPTER XV

THE PEARL RING

THERE had been a few days of clear, warm autumn weather, the sort of weather that inspired the Dana girls and their chums to plan a picnic for the coming Saturday.

Jean, Louise, and Evelyn had been chosen as a committee to select a location for the outing, and with this in view they set out one afternoon for Maple Grove, a mile off the main highway near Starhurst.

"I know the very place!" Evelyn had said. "There is a little clearing in the grove, just a few yards away from the side road. Franklin and I used to go there years ago. I'll show you the place, and you won't want to hold the picnic anywhere else."

The afternoon was beautiful, and the girls hiked across country from the school grounds. Guided by Evelyn, they made their way toward the proposed picnic spot. Before they came within sight of the clearing, Louise stopped, listening.

"I think I hear people talking," she said.

The girls halted beneath the trees. A dull

123

murmur of voices reached their ears. Then came the sharp outcry of a woman:

"I won't let you have it. I tell you, it's mine!"

Evelyn frowned.

"I wonder who can be at the picnic place. People don't often come here."

The girls went on quietly. To Jean and Louise that woman's voice had sounded strangely familiar. Then, as they drew closer to the clearing, they heard the sharp tones again.

"I'm not telling you where I got it. That's none of your business."

Jean grasped her sister's arm.

"Fay Violette!" she whispered excitedly.

Louise nodded. Cautiously she led the way, and a moment later the girls came within sight of the clearing.

A man and a woman stood facing each other in the open patch of ground, littered with dry autumn leaves. The woman was indeed Fay Violette.

An involuntary cry broke from Jean's lips when she recognized the man. He was Jake Garbone!

The secondhand dealer was evidently in a bad temper. He was arguing passionately with the fortune teller, gesticulating with his fat hands.

"I want that ring, do you hear? I know

where you got it. I've seen a description of
that ring. The police are looking for it. You
stole it from Mrs. Grantland.''

"What of it?" asked Fay Violette sullenly.

"I'll sell it for you and give you half the
money.''

The woman laughed harshly.

"You've told me that story before. I know
how much of the money I'd see. None of it.''

"Now listen here, Fay," said the man in an
ingratiating voice. "Aren't we brother and
sister? Do you mean to say you wouldn't
trust your own brother?"

"No!"

Jake Garbone shrugged. "A fine way to
talk!" he said. "Let me see the ring.''

Fay fumbled in her handbag and held out
an object in the palm of her hand. Jake Garbone studied it for a moment, then shook his
head.

"It is not worth much," he said. "I'll give
you a hundred dollars for it.''

"You'll give me five hundred," snapped his
sister. "It's worth a thousand.''

"Five hundred!" howled Jake Garbone.
"You must think I'm crazy.''

"Then I'll keep it.''

"I don't like the way you've been acting
lately," snarled Garbone. "You've even
changed your name. Are you ashamed of *our*
name?"

"I'm through working with you. I'm out on my own now."

"Much good it will do you! When you left me, what did you do? You took that lamp and sold it."

"I didn't."

"You did. I went to the trouble of stealing that lamp from the Danas' house and then you took it away before I had a chance to make any money out of it."

"You told me to take it away. You were afraid those girls would have the police search the store. I thought you meant me to sell it."

"Where is it now?"

"The Dana girls have it."

The sisters, hiding behind a clump of brush, were almost breathless with excitement.

"How did they get it?" yelled Jake. "Did you sell it back to them?"

"No. I took it to a dealer and they saw it in his window. When I knew you didn't want the lamp sold, I tried to get it back. I offered them more than they paid for it, but they refused."

"You've bungled the whole business from beginning to end," stormed Jake Garbone. "You sold that lamp when you had no right to sell it. I ran all kinds of risks stealing it in the first place. You didn't even give me the money you got for it——"

"I tried to get it back."

"But you didn't! Do those girls know it's their own lamp?"

"No."

"There's that to be thankful for, then. And now I want that ring! It'll pay me back a little for what you've cost me."

"I won't give you the ring. It's mine and I'm going to keep it unless you give me five hundred dollars for it."

"Give it to me!" snarled Jake Garbone, striding toward the woman. She thrust her hand behind her back. For a moment the pair wrestled, the dealer fighting to take the piece of jewelry from his sister. Suddenly, with a cry of rage, he clenched his fist and struck her in the face. She screamed. As he struck her again, she staggered back and tumbled to the ground. Jake Garbone pulled her fingers apart and snatched the ring from her hand.

This was too much. Horrified, the three girls had gazed at the extraordinary scene. Then Louise, with a cry of anger, rushed out from among the trees, closely followed by Jean and Evelyn.

Jake Garbone looked up in amazement and fear. When he saw the three girls running toward him across the clearing, he took to his heels and made off down a small path that led to the side road.

"After him!" cried Louise. "He has Mrs. Grantland's ring!"

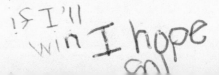
is I'll win I hope so!

For the moment Fay Violette was forgotten as the girls gave chase.

Jake Garbone, fat and pudgy, lumbered down the path. In plain sight, parked beside the road, was a sleek, dark brown coupé, which the man was hoping to reach before the girls should overtake him.

He was scrambling into the seat just as they reached the end of the path. The engine of the car was roaring. In another instant Jake Garbone would be speeding off down the road. Louise leaped across the ditch and ran out into the road directly in front of the car.

The coupé leaped forward, but the girl held her ground. Jake Garbone, raging, gestured frantically. He was a rascal, but he knew better than to deliberately run down the girl. He threw the clutch into reverse, and the car backed slowly. But there was a steep grade and the engine stalled.

In the meantime Jean and Evelyn had reached the running board and were desperately trying to force open the door of the car. Jake Garbone saw that he was in a predicament. With an angry imprecation he flung open the door on the opposite side, leaped out into the road, and went plunging into the bushes across the way.

The girls resumed their pursuit, but in the heavy shrubbery Jake Garbone was soon lost to view.

"We'll never catch him!" cried Jean. "And we'd probably get hurt if we did."

They realized that even three girls would be no match for a desperate and powerful man. Satisfied that they had at least put the scoundrel to rout, they gave up the chase and returned to the road. Evelyn was openly anxious about Fay Violette.

"I'm sure he knocked her unconscious!" she declared. "She didn't stir after she fell to the ground."

"It was the most brutal thing I've ever seen in my life!" said Jean hotly.

When they returned to the clearing they found the victim of Jake Garbone's unwarranted attack lying where she had fallen senseless on the ground. The girls were horrified. So faint was the woman's breathing that they feared she had been seriously hurt.

"We'll have to get her to Penfield right away!" decided Louise. "If we go for a doctor, it may be too late."

"But Penfield is two miles away!" said Evelyn. "How can we carry her that distance?"

"There's Jake Garbone's car," suggested Jean.

"I'll drive it," said Louise. "Come! We'll carry her."

With considerable difficulty the girls managed to lift the unconscious woman from the ground and bring her out to the road. They realized the need of haste, for they were greatly alarmed by her failure to revive from the effects of the blow. She had fallen, they discovered, upon a large flat rock, and Jean voiced the suggestion that her skull might have been fractured by the impact.

With Louise at the wheel and the unconscious Fay Violette placed in the car, they discovered that in his efforts to escape Jake Garbone had backed the coupé dangerously close to a deep ditch. One rear wheel had sunk into the sand, and for a time every effort to get the car under way met with failure.

Jean sprang out and piled brush and rocks beneath the tire. Again the engine roared as Louise stepped on the accelerator. This time the tire gripped firmly, and the coupé lurched ahead out onto the hard surface of the road.

Louise was anxious, as the delay had cost valuable time. She felt that every moment was precious. The moment Jean scrambled back into the car and slammed the door the coupé jumped ahead.

"Oh, dear, I hope we're not too late!" said Evelyn.

They sped madly down the rough side road toward the highway. Louise gripped the wheel tensely, her mind full of a wild confusion of thoughts. Jake Garbone and Fay Violette were brother and sister! Fay Violette had

stolen Mrs. Grantland's ring! The study lamp
they had bought in Penfield was the same lamp
that had been stolen from them in Oak Falls!
They had learned much from that strange meeting in the woods.

CHAPTER XVI

The Stolen Car

Once out on the highway Louise paid scant attention to the speed regulations. Ordinarily she was a careful and law-abiding driver, but in this emergency she clung to the wheel of the swaying car and watched the speedometer jump to forty, to fifty, and finally to sixty miles an hour.

Fay Violette was still unconscious. Jean and Evelyn protected her from the jolting and bouncing of the car as well as they could, but were worried by her prolonged insensibility.

"We'd better take her to the hospital!" cried Jean.

Louise nodded. Although the vehicle was strange to her, she handled it expertly enough. They were already close to the outskirts of Penfield, and traffic was becoming heavier. She did not slow down, however.

Suddenly with a clatter and a roar a motorcycle shot alongside and a traffic officer signalled curtly.

The coupé slackened speed and Louise pulled in to the side of the road. The policeman clambered off his machine, drew a notebook from his pocket, and came over.

"Ever hear of such a thing as a speed limit?"

"We're in a dreadful hurry!" explained Louise.

"You were," he agreed. "I had to hit sixty to catch you at all."

"We're taking a woman to the hospital," said Louise desperately. "She's badly hurt. A man hit her. She may be dying."

The officer looked into the coupé. When he saw the white face of Fay Violette he whistled softly.

"That's different," he said quickly. He thrust his notebook back into his pocket. "All right, girls! I'll lead the way in."

He climbed back on his wheel. With the siren of the motorcycle shrieking steadily, he sped on into Penfield, clearing the way through the traffic while the coupé raced along behind. Thus escorted, the girls suffered no further delay and soon came within sight of the great brick buildings of Penfield Hospital. There, with the help of the policeman, they removed the unconscious woman from the car and gave her into the care of the hospital authorities.

A brisk and efficient reception clerk came over to Louise.

"The patient's name, please?"

"Why—she calls herself Fay Violette."

"Your name and address?"

The girls gave their names and explained that they were from Starhurst School.

"Very well," said the clerk, as she wrote down the details. "Is the patient a relative?"

"No," said Louise hastily. "We just happened to find her. A man struck her."

The officer then sought further details.

"Where did this happen?" he demanded. "Do you know the man's name?"

Louise faltered. She did not care to reveal too much about Fay Violette, Jake Garbone, and the affair of the study lamp. The more persistently the policeman questioned her, the more nervous she became. He frowned.

"You're trying to cover something up," he said. "You haven't told me the whole story."

Suddenly he stepped around to the back of the coupé, glanced at the number plate, then produced his notebook again. He perused a list of numbers.

"I thought so," he declared grimly.

"You thought what?" asked Jean.

"This is a stolen car. It was reported to the department three hours ago. You girls had better come down to Headquarters with me."

"But we didn't steal it!" said Louise indignantly. "The man ran away and left the car. We had to get the woman to the hospital——"

"That's all very well," returned the officer. "You'll have to tell your story to the captain."

Again under motorcycle escort the girls were

forced to drive away, but not before they learned from the hospital clerk that Fay Violette had recovered consciousness and was found to be in no immediate danger.

"Do you think they'll put us in jail?" quavered Evelyn.

"They wouldn't dare," replied Jean. "We haven't done anything wrong. If this is a stolen car, they ought to thank us for recovering it. But just the same we'll have to do a lot of explaining to Mrs. Crandall."

"I can almost see the newspaper headlines," groaned Louise. "'Starhurst Students Accused of Car Stealing.' Won't that be lovely?"

The girls were nervous as they stepped from the car in front of police headquarters. They did not blame the motorcycle officer, realizing that the man was merely doing his duty, but it was not comforting to know that they were suspected of having stolen the car.

"Just our luck!" said Jean dismally. "Jake Garbone helped himself to that car and now we'll be blamed for it."

The policeman led them up the steps. Just as they were entering the building, they encountered a familiar figure.

"Why, it's the plumber!" gasped Jean.

Looking shy and embarrassed, the mysterious workman spoke to them.

"Is there—anything wrong?"

"I should say so!" declared Louise. "We're

accused of stealing a car. But we are entirely innocent. We took it so we could bring a woman to the hospital, and then the officer found that it had been reported stolen."

The plumber turned to the officer.

"I can vouch for these girls," he said sharply. "They are from Starhurst School. They wouldn't think of doing such a thing."

"Well," said the man, "if you can put in a good word for them, it ought to go a long way with the captain. The coupé has been recovered, see, and it's my duty to bring them in to explain how they happened to be driving it."

"We'll settle that quickly enough," said the plumber.

He was as good as his word. When the girls were brought into headquarters, he spoke to a red-faced, gray-haired officer behind a high desk.

"Casey," he said, "these girls are from Starhurst School. They were found driving a car listed as stolen. I'll vouch for their respectability."

Casey smiled at the frightened girls.

"You don't look like auto thieves," he assured them. Then, turning to the motorcycle officer, he said:

"What's the story?"

The traffic policeman explained how he had overtaken the speeding car, but on learning that the girls were bringing an injured woman to the hospital, had given them what help he could.

"When I took a look at the license plate and saw it was a stolen car, I had to bring them in," he said.

"We didn't know it was stolen," insisted Louise. "You see, we were out at the Grove and saw this man Jake Garbone——"

"What's that?" demanded Casey, startled.

"Jake Garbone!" cried the plumber, vastly excited.

Mention of the secondhand dealer's name created something of a sensation. The girls were soon enlightened.

"Why, we've been trying to get hold of that crook for months," declared Casey. "Go ahead, Miss. Tell me what happened."

Louise gave her story, although she omitted mentioning the study lamp and the ring, merely saying that Jake Garbone and Fay Violette had been quarreling about stolen property. Prompted at intervals by Jean and Evelyn, she told how Jake had felled the woman to the ground and how he had made good his escape.

"Escaped, did he?" glowered Casey. "Well, if he's hanging around Penfield, we can make it hot for him. There's no doubt that Jake Garbone stole that car. We've been trying to catch him so we can question him about the theft of heirlooms from the Starr family some time ago."

"The Starr family?" exclaimed Evelyn. When Casey looked at her inquiringly, she introduced herself.

"So you're Miss Evelyn Starr!" he said. "Well, you may have heard that some heirlooms were stolen from your home before—well, before it became Starhurst School."

"Yes," she admitted. "I've heard my brother speak of the affair."

"We traced some of those valuables to Jake Garbone, but we were never able to collar the man himself. Now, if you'll excuse me for a minute——"

Casey hurried away. After a while he returned and said that instructions had been issued for an immediate search.

"I hope you catch him!" declared the plumber. "The man's an out-and-out rascal. He should be behind bars."

"Do you know him?" inquired Jean, interested.

"I've heard of him. I hope the police catch him. The man should have been in prison long ago."

The girls were surprised at the workman's evident eagerness for Jake Garbone's arrest. At that moment, however, Casey interrupted to apologize for any inconvenience they might have suffered and to thank them for the information they had given him.

"You've done us a great service in putting

us on Jake Garbone's trail again," he said.
"As for the stolen car, we'll take care that the
owner learns who was responsible for its return."

The girls left police headquarters in company with the plumber. At the foot of the
steps they thanked him for his help.

"It's very fortunate that we met you," said
Louise. "The police might have made it unpleasant for us if you hadn't identified us."

The man looked more embarrassed than ever.
He raised his hat.

"That's quite all right," he said. "It was a
pleasure. I—I hope I see you again."

"Perhaps he'll invite you to the Plumbers'
Ball," broke in a familiar, disagreeable voice.

Jean looked up and to her mortification saw
Lettie Briggs and Ina Mason walking past.
Recalling Lettie's malicious remarks concerning her interest in the plumber, Jean felt that
the pair could not have chosen a more inoppor-
tune time to appear.

"Quite a little romance!" sneered Lettie.

CHAPTER XVII

The Campus Spy

"They *would* happen along just at this time!" said Jean, after Lettie and Ina had gone by.

Evelyn shrugged.

"Don't worry about them," she advised.

A policeman came out of headquarters at that moment. He smiled at the girls, touching his cap. He opened the door of the coupé.

"The owner of this car will be glad to see it again," he grinned.

As he drove away, Louise frowned.

"I wonder if Jake Garbone got away with Mrs. Grantland's ring after all," she said slowly.

"I'm afraid he did," said Evelyn. "He certainly snatched it out of Fay Violette's hand. We saw him."

"But did he *keep* it?" argued Louise. "It occurs to me that we haven't been very clever. He may have hidden that ring under the car cushions."

Evelyn looked crestfallen.

"And we never thought to look!"

"It occurred to me to do that very thing," said Jean calmly. "While you were breaking the speed records on the Penfield highway, I felt beneath the cushions."

"And you didn't find the ring?"

Jean held out her hand.

"Look!"

There, in her palm, was the pearl ring.

Evelyn and Louise were instantly excited.

"You found it!" they cried. "You found Mrs. Grantland's ring!"

They examined the beautiful jewel while Jean smiled happily. She had, she explained, a "hunch" that Jake Garbone had concealed the ornament somewhere in the car because he would not run the risk of having the stolen object on his person if he were caught.

"Luckily I found it before the police claimed the coupé," she said. "Now let's go and return the ring to Mrs. Grantland."

Joyously the trio set out for Mrs. Grantland's home. Louise had the address, having jotted it down when that lady had suggested that they might call at her home some afternoon. Within ten minutes they were approaching a handsome residence on one of Penfield's finest streets.

To their astonishment they saw the brown coupé standing at the curb in front of the Grantland home. Talking to the policeman who had driven away from Headquarters in the car were Mrs. Grantland and a stout, pleasant-faced man who could be none other than Mr. Grantland himself.

"Why, here you are!" exclaimed the middle-aged lady excitedly. "This policeman has just returned our car. He told us that three girls had recovered it——"

"Those are the girls, all right," said the officer. "They were almost held for stealing the machine."

Mr. Grantland extended his hand.

"Are these the young ladies I've been hearing about? If you won't introduce me, Emma, I'll introduce myself. Grantland's my name and I want to tell you how much I'm obliged to you. My wife told me that you had considerable talent for detective work, but I didn't expect to have it proved to me in this fashion."

He shook hands with the girls and told them that the car had been purchased the previous morning.

"I tell you," he said, "I didn't relish the thought of losing that coupé within twenty-four hours of paying out two thousand dollars cash for it. I didn't even have time to put theft insurance on it, so it would have been a dead loss."

"You must come into the house and tell us all about it," insisted Mrs. Grantland, as she led the girls up the walk.

"But first of all we have something else to

show you," said Louise, smiling. "We can't
take much credit for recovering the car. That
was more or less accidental. But Jean has
something that should interest you."

Quietly Jean handed Mrs. Grantland the
bit of jewelry.

"My ring! My pearl ring!" she cried in
excitement. "Tom, look! They've brought
back my ring."

Mr. Grantland stared at the circlet, then at
the girls.

"Well, all I have to say," he observed
slowly, "is that you beat the city detective
bureau all hollow. A ring and a car—all in
one day!"

Mrs. Grantland's delight was unbounded, for
the loss of her precious possession had been a
severe blow to her. In the house she insisted
on hearing every detail of the story, and her
admiration of their pluck and astuteness was
expressed in no uncertain terms. Mr. Grantland expressed his conviction that they were
the cleverest girls he had ever known.

However, a rude shock awaited them when
they returned to Starhurst School half an hour
later. They had scarcely entered the building
before an excited freshman rushed up to them.

"Dana girls are wanted in the office!" she
gasped.

"What's wrong?" asked Jean in surprise.

"Mrs. Crandall has fire in her eye," the

freshman warned them. "Lettie Briggs told her you had been arrested and taken to the police station for stealing a car. I wouldn't be in your shoes right now for anything."

With considerable trepidation the girls went to the office. They realized that an ugly construction could be placed on the incident if Mrs. Crandall had heard only half the truth. The headmistress surveyed them grimly as they stood before her desk.

"Is it true that you girls were taken to the police station this afternoon?"

"Well—yes, we were, Mrs. Crandall," Louise admitted.

"On suspicion of stealing a car?"

"It was all a mistake," ventured Jean. "The car *had* been stolen——"

"You realize that such conduct does not help the reputation of Starhurst School," said Mrs. Crandall severely.

Before the girls could reply the telephone rang.

"One moment!" said Mrs. Crandall, as she answered the call.

There was a brief conversation. Mrs. Crandall's expression softened as she listened to the voice over the wire.

"Yes—I understand—that alters the situation a great deal—yes—thank you very much, Mrs. Grantland—certainly—good-bye."

She put aside the instrument.

"Mrs. Grantland has just explained the facts of the case," she said in a gentler voice. "I am afraid I did you an injustice, girls. It seems you are to be commended rather than scolded. Won't you tell me how it all happened?"

The girls reviewed their story. When they were finally dismissed by Mrs. Crandall, it was with a warm word of congratulation. Jean and Louise were greatly relieved and glad that Mrs. Grantland had intervened when she did, for the outcome might have been unpleasant.

That evening Evelyn Starr joined them in the study. She had made a practice of bringing her books to their room every evening and usually occupied herself quietly with her preparations for the next day's classes. She was an ambitious student, eager to make the most of her opportunities. But this evening she was restless and ill at ease.

"I just can't concentrate on my lessons!" she said. "I try and try, but it's no use."

Louise put a sympathetic arm around the girl.

"You must not worry so much, dear. It doesn't help. Everything will come out all right, I'm sure."

"I can't keep from worrying," said Evelyn. "I know it's foolish—but if you had no one left in the world except your brother—and he dropped out of sight——"

Her voice choked as she tried to fight back the tears.

"I have scarcely a cent left," she confessed. "I've spent so much money on telephone calls and telegrams—even cables—trying to find a trace of him. I'm going to ask Mrs. Crandall if she will let me wait on tables in the dining hall."

"Evelyn! Is it that bad?" exclaimed Louise, shocked. "Won't you let us help? We can lend you some money."

Evelyn shook her head in refusal, but the Dana girls insisted. Although Uncle Ned was not wealthy, he gave them a liberal allowance of pocket money.

"If you won't let us lend you this, we'll be angry," declared Louise, taking a five-dollar bill from her purse. "Now you *must* take it, Evelyn!"

"What's the fun of having friends if you can't give a helping hand once in a while?" said Jean. "You would do it for us quickly enough if we were in trouble."

Evelyn finally consented to accept the money, on the strict understanding that she would repay it as soon as she could.

"It's very good of you," she said gratefully. "I wouldn't accept it if I didn't really need it."

At that moment Jean, who had sauntered over to the window, said sharply:

"Girls! Come here—quickly!"

They rushed to the aperture. Jean pointed down to the campus below.

"Look! That man again!"

In the lamplight that streamed through the window they caught a glimpse of a skulking figure beneath the trees.

Had the campus spy returned?

CHAPTER XVIII

TRYING TO HELP

THE watcher did not remain long beneath the window. The moment he realized that he had been seen, he withdrew quickly into the deeper shadows of the trees. The girls had a glimpse of his furtive figure stealing off across the campus and then disappearing.

"Let's follow him!" exclaimed Jean in excitement.

"We'd never catch him," replied Louise. "He knows we saw him."

"Do you think," asked Evelyn anxiously, "it is—the same man——?"

They knew the thought that was in her mind; that the spy was none other than Franklin Starr.

Jean's brow wrinkled.

"Somehow," she declared, "I think this was another man altogether. He seemed shorter and stouter."

Louise agreed with her.

"It's my idea," she said, "that this man was Jake Garbone!"

The girls looked at one another in momentary silence. The possibility that the fugitive had ventured to the very walls of Starhurst was alarming. The cruel dealer was a reckless and determined man.

"Perhaps he hopes to get the ring again," said Jean. "I don't like to think of that fellow being so close."

"He should be locked up!" insisted Louise. "We'll have to be on our guard. He may have come here in hopes of stealing the lamp."

They could not understand Garbone's obvious determination to get possession of the study lamp. Knowing, as they now did, that it was the one given them by Uncle Ned, it was doubly precious to them. For some reason the wily dealer coveted it.

Jean went over to the table and thoughtfully regarded the beautiful piece of hammered metal.

"Uncle Ned said it was an antique. Perhaps it is a great deal more valuable than he thought. Jake Garbone may have known something about it."

After much discussion they finally decided to say nothing to the Crandalls about their suspicion that Garbone was hanging around the school, but they resolved to devote every bit of energy toward bringing the dealer to justice. The longer the man stayed in the vicinity of Penfield, the more risk he ran of being captured by the police.

"If we have any talent as amateur detectives," laughed Jean, "we ought to be able to catch him ourselves."

"As for the lamp," Louise declared, "we had better watch it carefully from now on. I don't know why it's so valuable to that man, but he's not going to have it."

After Evelyn had gone back to her own room that evening, Jean suggested a plan of campaign.

"Maybe Fay Violette will be able to give us some information. Isn't it likely that she will know where Garbone is hiding?"

"Would she tell us?"

"Why not? She'll have no love for him now —even if he is her brother. We practically saved her life. At least she might tell us why he is so determined to get possession of the lamp."

Louise agreed that the fortune teller might be disposed to help them.

"Let's go to the hospital tomorrow and talk to her. I'm afraid she won't be inclined to tell us very much, however. If she has been stealing for Garbone, she'll be afraid of getting herself into trouble."

Next day at luncheon the Dana girls had a shock. Evelyn Starr was not at her usual place at the table. Instead she came in from the kitchen, waiting on the other girls, her face set and white. It was plain that she felt her position keenly. There was a whispered buzz of conversation the moment she left the dining hall.

"Quite a comedown for the heiress of Starhurst!" sneered Lettie Briggs. "I wonder that she has the impudence to stay at school. I wouldn't wait on table—not if I never had an education."

"No," said Louise calmly. "It takes courage."

Lettie flashed her an angry glance but for the duration of the meal remained silent and had no further remarks to make about Evelyn.

After luncheon the Dana girls sought out their chum. Tactfully they made it clear to her that they admired her bravery.

"But it really isn't necessary," said Louise. "We'll be more than glad to lend you any money you need."

Evelyn shook her head.

"I'd rather fight my own way," she said proudly. "If I can't do that, I'll leave school. I know you mean to be kind, but I can't keep on borrowing. Waiting on table isn't so bad, anyway. We have lots of fu in the kitchen."

The Dana girls wished they could do something to help her, but they realized that only one thing could help Evelyn: her brother must be found.

"We'll send a telegram to Uncle Ned!" decided Louise.

They went up to their study. After several attempts they composed a message to their uncle. It read:

> PLEASE WIRE IF YOU KNOW WHEREABOUTS OF FRANKLIN STARR HAS BEEN MISSING SINCE HE LEFT OAK FALLS HIS SISTER GREATLY WORRIED CAN YOU HELP

Jean volunteered to take the message to the telegraph office.

"He may have written to Uncle Ned," said Louise. "At any rate, it doesn't do any harm to make inquiries, and we may learn something of interest."

"Let's hope so," replied Jean, as she folded the message and put it in her purse. "And I do hope we receive an answer soon."

CHAPTER XIX

THE SECRET PANEL

WHEN Jean left to take the message to the telegraph office, Louise sat down at her desk to study. For a while she found it difficult to concentrate on her work, for her mind was filled with thoughts of Evelyn Starr's troubles and of the mysterious activities of Jake Garbone. Again and again her eyes were drawn to the study lamp. What was the mystery about it? Why was Jake Garbone so set upon regaining possession of it?

Eventually, however, she settled down to her lessons and worked busily for a time until she was disturbed by a knock at the door.

"Come in," she called.

The door opened. Louise looked up to confront the mysterious plumber and one of the housemaids. Politely he ducked his head, gazing at her through his spectacles.

"Sorry to disturb you, Miss," he said awkwardly, "but I have to test the radiator pipes."

"All right," replied Louise, bending over her books again. "It's no bother."

The workman silently crossed the room. For

a while there was no sound but the tap-tapping
of a hammer upon the pipes.

"You helped us out of a bad fix yesterday,"
said Louise, looking up.

"I didn't do much," replied the plumber, still
busy with the pipes. "The police should have
known you didn't steal the car."

"We should have had a great deal of explaining to do if you hadn't made it easier for us,
just the same."

"I'm very glad if I was of any help," said
the man quietly.

Louise went on with her work. She was
puzzled by this strange individual. His very
appearance was odd, for although he had a
light mustache, his hair was jet black. After
a while she noticed that the tapping had ceased.

She glanced over the top of her book, but the
plumber did not realize that he was being observed. He stood gazing intently at the study
lamp. For several moments he remained there,
and in all that time his earnest gaze did not
once leave the object. He seemed entirely oblivious of everything else.

"You seem very interested in our light,"
said Louise finally.

The plumber was startled. He dropped his
hammer and bent over quickly to pick it up.
There was a shamefaced, frightened expression
on his countenance when he looked at Louise
Dana again.

"I—I—well—it's a very beautiful lamp," he stammered.

"Why are you so interested in it?" persisted Louise.

"Interested?"

"Yes. After all, it's merely a lamp. Is there anything particularly fascinating about it?"

"Why, no," he said. "Nothing special. I was just looking at it. I—I like lamps."

"This is an antique."

"Yes. Excuse me. I didn't mean to be rude. I—I guess I'd better be going."

Hastily he turned away. In his embarrassment he tripped over a corner of the rug, stumbled, and almost fell. To save himself, he thrust out his hand and steadied himself against the wall.

His fingers struck a loose panel in the woodwork. He straightened up, glancing sharply at the board that had given slightly beneath the impact. Louise had not noticed the movable part in the wall, but she did see that the plumber became strangely alert.

"Very clumsy of me," he muttered.

At that moment there came from outdoors the voices of a number of the Dana girls' school chums, calling from the campus below.

"Louise! Oh, Louise!"

She went over to the window and looked out. Doris, Ann, and a number of the other girls were standing beneath it.

"We're getting up a game of volley ball. Come and play for our side."

"I'll be right down," Louise promised.

She stood at the window for no more than a few seconds, her back turned to the plumber. The brief respite was enough for the man. His arm flashed out. He drew the loose board quickly aside and reached into the aperture. His hand emerged, grasping a bundle of dusty papers. A swift motion and he had closed the panel again. Then, thrusting the papers inside his coat, he hurried out of the room.

When Louise turned away from the window she recalled the sudden change in the plumber's demeanor as he had steadied himself against the wall.

"I wonder," she said to herself, and went over to examine the woodwork.

It has already been noted that there was one secret cupboard in the study. Now, as Louise looked closely at the panelling, she saw that the hidden recess they already knew was matched by another of which they had no inkling. The panel had been thrust back so hastily that it did not fit accurately into position. It was strange, she reflected, that they had never noticed the tiny crack in the woodwork before.

Curious, she moved back the board. It revealed a tiny cupboard in the wall, about a foot deep. She peered inside, but the secret enclosure was empty.

"No wonder he looked startled," she said to herself. "He must have felt the panel move."

Louise had no suspicion, however, that the plumber had actually discovered the secret cupboard and removed its contents.

"It *is* strange that we didn't notice that loose partition before this."

She locked the study door and went down to the campus, dismissing the matter of the sliding panel from her mind.

Jean's journey to the telegraph office should not have taken more than half an hour at the most, but when Louise returned to the study almost two hours later she was surprised to find that her sister had not returned. Puzzled by Jean's prolonged absence, she was about to inquire among the other students, when there was a rush of flying feet in the corridor, the door burst open, and Jean dashed into the room.

"Where on earth—?" began Louise.

"Come on!" gasped Jean, her cheeks flushed, her eyes sparkling with excitement. "I've found him!"

She grabbed Louise by the hand and fairly dragged her out of the study.

"Found whom? Not Franklin Starr?"

"No! Jake Garbone!"

"Where?" demanded Louise, as they rushed pell-mell down the stairs.

"At the picnic grounds. If we hurry we may see him again," she said breathlessly.

Hurriedly she explained. Upon finding the study door locked on her return to the school, Jean had acted "on a hunch" and gone for a hike to the Grove. There, in the very clearing where they had seen the rascally secondhand dealer quarreling with Fay Violette, she had caught a glimpse of Jake Garbone.

"He was looking for something. Searching every inch of the ground. I hurried back as quickly as I could."

"Did he see you?"

Jean shook her head.

"I took good care that he didn't."

"Don't you think we had better tell the police?" Louise suggested.

"He may be gone by now. Then we *would* look foolish. They might think I had never seen him at all. I have a better idea. Let's try to borrow Mrs. Grantland's car. We can drive out to the Grove in a few minutes. If we see Garbone, we may be able to follow him and learn where he has been hiding."

"Perhaps he came back to look for the ring," Louise suggested as they fled down the school steps.

"I think it was something else. He must have deliberately hidden the ring behind the car cushions. He wouldn't be looking for it at the picnic grounds."

They were curious to know what had drawn Jake Garbone back to the place in question.

their minds set upon catching sight of him and locating his hiding place if they could. When they reached Mrs. Grantland's house they explained the situation to her.

"You're more than welcome to use my car," she told them. "But aren't you afraid?"

"Afraid of what?" laughed Jean.

"Well—I know I'd think twice before going after that sort of man, without at least a dozen policemen," said Mrs. Grantland.

"He won't see us if we can avoid it," Louise explained.

Mrs. Grantland was dubious. She advised them to notify the police, but the girls felt that the authorities might only succeed in frightening away their quarry.

"If we can discover where he is hiding," said Jean, "we can tell the police."

"Do be careful," begged Mrs. Grantland nervously. "I really don't mind lending you the car. You're welcome to use it any time you wish, but I should never forgive myself if it got you into any trouble."

"Don't worry about us, Mrs. Grantland," said Louise. "We don't intend to take any chances."

Time was pressing, so they thanked their friend warmly, got quickly into the coupé and drove away. Louise, at the wheel, guided the car skillfully through the town traffic until at last they were speeding along the highway out of Penfield. The girls were tense with excitement.

"I do hope we haven't lost too much time!" said Jean. "He may be gone by now."

The car leaped ahead as Louise pressed down the accelerator.

"We'll soon know."

In a few minutes they were in sight of the road that led toward the Grove.

CHAPTER XX

The Clue of the Watch

The car ascended the hillside road. It was late afternoon by now and the light was failing. The Dana girls realized that darkness would soon cut short their search for Jake Garbone.

"Suppose he comes out to the road while we're gone?" said Jean. "He might steal the coupé."

"We'll lock it. We shan't be far away in any case."

Louise took the precaution to turn the vehicle around when they came to the place in the road nearest the picnic grounds.

"If we have to run for it, we won't have to waste time heading the car back toward the highway," she explained.

As soon as Louise had parked the car, the girls entered the path under the trees. In the fading light, with the dry branches creaking overhead and dead leaves skittering at their feet, the atmosphere of the Grove was sinister.

"It won't do to let him see us," whispered Louise.

Step by step they advanced until they came in sight of the clearing. The girls stood behind a clump of trees, watching the open space of the picnic ground. The clearing was deserted.

"He's gone!" breathed Jean, disappointed.

"Don't be too sure. We can explore the place, anyway."

They knew that there was a possibility that Jake Garbone might be hidden somewhere among the trees on the opposite side, so they did not relax their caution. Carefully they made their way out into the grounds.

"I wonder what he was looking for?" murmured Louise.

"Whatever it was, he might not have found it, you know."

The girls searched through the dry grass. It was Jean's theory that the pudgy dealer had lost something in his flight from the place after his brutal attack upon his sister.

"It must have been important or valuable," she insisted, "otherwise he wouldn't have come back to look for it. I'm sure it wasn't the ring. He hid that deliberately under the cushions, and when he lost the car he knew he had lost the ring too."

For some time they searched, but without success.

"Nearly sundown," said Louise, straightening up. "I'm afraid we're on a wild-goose chase, Jean."

Jean surveyed the open space of autumn grass.

"We haven't covered a quarter of the ground yet," she sighed.

At that moment the setting sun broke through a bank of clouds, its gleaming rays slanting through the branches of the trees which bordered the clearing. From a patch of turf only a few yards away came a golden gleam of light, revealing some shiny object on the ground.

"What can that be?" cried Jean. She ran toward it, knelt down, and picked it up. Then she uttered a cry of delight.

"A watch! A gold watch!"

Together the Dana girls examined the timepiece, which proved to be a heavy, old-fashioned watch in a case of solid gold.

"That's what he was looking for!" exclaimed Louise.

"Probably stolen."

Jean turned the object over in her hands.

"I suppose we could trace the owner through the number of the watch," she said thoughtfully.

The girls were elated by their discovery, but as yet did not realize its full importance.

Louise had an inspiration. Quickly she began to unfasten the back of the case.

"There may be a photograph, or a name——"

When the girls looked at the inside they saw

an engraved inscription that brought a gasp of astonishment to their lips, for it read:

"*To Franklin Starr—from his father.*"

Jean looked up, her eyes bewildered.

"To Franklin Starr!" she exclaimed.

Louise was equally surprised.

"I can't understand it."

"Can it mean that Franklin Starr has been *here?*" said Jean.

"But Jake Garbone was looking for something. It must have been this watch," Louise pointed out. "He must be connected, somehow, with Franklin Starr.

"What could they have in common?" cried Jean. "And yet—you remember—when Franklin Starr saw Garbone on the station platform at Oak Falls, he recognized him. Tried to follow him onto the train."

"I wonder," Louise said slowly, "if Jake Garbone had anything to do with Franklin Starr's disappearance."

The mystery that surrounded Evelyn's brother was deeper than ever. Why had he been so confused and excited when he recognized Jake Garbone at the railroad station? Why had he left the Dana home so suddenly? Why had he vanished without a word of explanation to his sister and his friends? And how had his watch come into Jake Garbone's possession?

"Perhaps," said Louise, answering her sister's unspoken thought, "Franklin Starr sold the watch to Garbone."

"But it was given to him by his father. He wouldn't sell that sort of gift. And he wouldn't pawn it," argued Jean. "I can't under-stand——"

At that moment they were aroused by the sharp noise of a snapped twig. They looked up.

The clearing was deserted except for themselves. Suddenly, through the bare branches of a clump of stunted trees not more than a few yards away, Louise saw a human face! It was the face of Jake Garbone!

The cruel eyes of the rascally dealer stared at the girls from beyond the network of branches. Then the man plunged forward, thrusting aside the twigs, and strode out into the clearing. There was unutterable menace in his face as he came slowly toward the girls.

Escape by the path to the road was barred. Unarmed, the Danas knew they could not cope with the man.

"You have found my watch," he said, while he was still a few feet away. "Give it to me!"

He extended a fat hand. Jean thrust the timepiece behind her back.

"It isn't yours," she replied bravely.

"It is mine, I tell you," Garbone retorted, an angry light in his eyes. "Give it to me at once!"

"It belongs to Franklin Starr!" declared

Louise with spirit. "His name is on the case. How did it ever come into your hands?"

Jake Garbone did not answer in words. Instead, with a snarl of anger, he leaped forward, hoping to snatch the watch from Jean's grasp.

She was too quick for him, however. She sprang aside, and at the same time Louise thrust her foot out. Garbone tripped and fell heavily to the ground.

"Run!" cried Louise.

The girls fled across the clearing. They were only a few yards from the trees bordering the picnic grounds, and by the time the man had scrambled to his feet the Danas were plunging through the undergrowth.

"It's mine!" yelled Garbone. "You'll give that watch back to me——"

The rest of the sentence was lost in his stuttered imprecations as he lumbered across the clearing in pursuit.

Jean was in the lead. She realized that their only hope lay in leaving the dealer behind them in the Grove. They had half a dozen yards' start, but the man was remarkably quick for all his weight, and anger spurred him on. Jean found a path among the maples, followed it for a short distance, then struck off down a branch trail that opened to one side. Her sister was close at her heels.

Louise glanced back. Garbone was plunging along down the path, not twenty feet behind

She lost sight of him a moment later beyond a dense screen of bushes. Jean darted down another bypath. Louise followed.

Suddenly Jean stopped, gripped her sister's arm tightly.

"Wait!" she whispered. "He can hear us when we're running."

A moment later they heard a great crashing among the bushes, followed by a puffing and panting as Jake Garbone ploughed on down the path. He missed the side trail entirely and went plunging ahead.

Then they heard a frightened shout. There was a roar, a clatter of falling rock, a howl of fear, then a succession of bumps and thuds.

"What on earth has happened?" gasped Jean in amazement.

"He must have tumbled over a cliff."

The girls ventured out onto the main path. They made their way cautiously ahead. Then they saw what had happened to Jake Garbone.

The path had ended on a steep hillside. In his blind pursuit the man had been unable to check himself. The loose earth and gravel at the end of the trail had given way and he had gone tumbling headlong down the slope. They could hear him groaning and cursing, twenty feet below.

They peered over the ledge. At the bottom of the declivity Jake Garbone was painfully picking himself up and brushing the sand and grime from his clothes. The girls knew that they were safe from him for the time being, as the slope afforded no foothold for a return climb.

"I'll get them!" they heard Garbone muttering. "I'll get that watch back or my name ain't Jake Garbone. Those girls are a long ways from Starhurst yet."

He had no intention of abandoning the pursuit. As they withdrew from the brink of the ledge, the Dana girls knew it would be only a matter of time before the dealer would find his way to the higher ground and take up the chase once more.

"We'd better get back to the road, quick!" declared Louise.

"If we can find our way to the clearing."

Twilight had fallen, and in the maze of paths they were confused, but by following one well-beaten trail they eventually reached the picnic grounds again. There they fled across the open space and raced down the path toward the road.

"I hope the coupé is still there!" panted Jean.

The car was parked where they had left it. Louise fumbled for the key.

"I've lost it!" she exclaimed frantically.

They were assailed by momentary panic. They knew that Garbone's first thought would be for the road. With trembling fingers Louise again explored her pocket.

"Don't tell me you can't find that key!" begged Jean.

"No—here it is—in the lining of my pocket!"

Joyously Louise unlocked the door, scrambled into the seat, and settled down behind the wheel. There was no time to lose. At any moment Jake Garbone might find his bearings and come plunging out onto the road.

Louise snapped on the ignition, pressed the starter. Instantly she knew there was something wrong, as the car did not respond. She tried again and again.

Suddenly she exclaimed:

"We're out of gasoline!"

CHAPTER XXI

THE INTRUDER

"OUT of gas?" groaned Jean. "Now we *are* in trouble. What's to be done?"

Louise was conscious of a momentary qualm of fear. On that gloomy road, with the rascally Garbone searching the bush for them, they were in a dangerous predicament. In an instant her quick wits leaped to a solution.

"Why didn't I think of it? We're on a grade. This path slopes to the highway. We can coast down!"

Jean flung open the door and leaped out into the road. With the brake released, only a slight push was necessary to get the car under way. As the tires slithered in the dust, Jean jumped onto the running board. The roadster began to move slowly down the incline. With gathering speed, as the brake pressure was relinquished, it rushed on downward. The shadowy trees flashed past. Louise gripped the wheel tightly.

"The highway slopes downhill all the way to Penfield!" she cried. "If we have enough speed when we leave this road, we'll be able to reach town."

With ever-increasing momentum the car shot forward. By the time the girls came within sight of the highway, at right angles to the side road, they were travelling at breakneck speed.

"I hope we shan't have to stop," cried Jean, "when we get to the main road."

"Don't see any cars, do you?" asked Louise excitedly.

Bumping and swaying, the coupé shot out onto the concrete surface. Luckily there was no traffic on either side at the moment, so Louise was not forced to stop. She swung desperately on the wheel the moment the front tires hit the smooth pavement. She had to act quickly or the car would have shot directly across and into the ditch on the far side.

At that, their escape was a narrow one. Only deft juggling of the steering apparatus averted disaster. The auto swung around, skidded, plunged toward the side of the road, then righted itself as Louise swung back the wheel. With all the momentum of its wild plunge down the slope the car whizzed toward the lights of Penfield.

"Shall we tell the police when we reach town?" asked Jean.

Louise nodded, her eyes fixed on the highway.

"Of course. If they catch him, they'll force him to tell what he knows about Franklin Starr."

Louise leaned suddenly forward. She had

seen a human figure scrambling up from the ditch at the side of the concrete stretch. The glare of the headlights shone clearly on him as he ran directly out into the middle of the road.

Her foot was almost on the brake when she recognized the man as Jake Garbone. His clothes were torn and covered with dust. Not fifty feet away he stood waving his arms, signalling them to stop.

She guessed that the man did not realize who were the occupants of the car. He had merely taken a chance on the first passing automobile he saw, hoping for a drive to town.

"Don't stop!" cried Jean.

Louise sounded a warning blast on the horn, not altering the course of her speeding car by a fraction of an inch. To her horror the man did not move. He stood right in their path. Then, when it seemed inevitable that Garbone must be hit, he jumped wildly aside.

The car flashed past as he sprawled on the highway. The girls breathed sighs of relief.

"We might have been in jail for manslaughter if we'd hit him," gasped Jean.

"I'm glad he had sense enough to jump."

The car rushed on. When they reached the level highway within the limits of Penfield, their speed diminished somewhat, but there were no hills to climb and they managed to coast on into the town. By the time they came within sight of a service station the car was barely crawling along.

"Just made it, eh?" grinned an attendant, coming out.

"I was never so glad to see a gas station before in all my life," Louise confessed.

The man filled up the tank and they drove on to police headquarters. There, to the good-natured officer at the desk, they told the story of their encounter with Jake Garbone. He listened attentively, then reached for a telephone and rapped out a brisk order.

"Tom!" he said to his unseen listener. "Garbone was seen out on the north highway a few minutes ago. Yes—trying to flag a ride into town. Have the boys check up on incoming cars. Take your motorcycle and go out there. Pick him up and bring him in. We want that fellow."

He replaced the receiver.

"Many thanks, girls. He's a slippery customer, this Garbone, but maybe we'll catch him this time."

He looked curiously at the watch, which they had shown him in telling of their adventure.

"You say this man Starr has been missing for several days? Garbone probably knows something about him. Either that, or he stole the watch before Starr disappeared. I hardly think he came by it honestly at any rate. Better leave the timepiece with us for a few days, and if Mr. Starr doesn't turn up, his sister can claim it.''

The girls agreed to this. As there was nothing else they could do by way of helping to locate the elusive Garbone, they drove back to Mrs. Grantland's house and returned the car. That lady was highly excited when they told her of their experience at the Grove.

''I declare, I don't think it was wise of me to let you have the coupé,'' she said nervously. ''You might have been killed.''

''Biggest thrill we've had in ages,'' laughed Jean.

''I do hope the police catch that man. He's a villain if there ever was one. How on earth did he get possession of Mr. Starr's watch?''

''When we know that,'' returned Louise seriously, ''I think we'll know what has happened to Franklin Starr.''

They left Mrs. Grantland and hurried back to the school. They took a short cut across the campus. Lights already shone from the study windows.

''Did you lock the door before we left?'' asked Jean. ''Every time we come back to the study I expect to find our lamp stolen.''

''That door stays locked whenever we're out,'' replied Louise. ''Unless Evelyn is in the study, of course,'' she added.

As they crossed beneath the campus trees they scanned the front of the massive building.

When they came in sight of their own window they saw that it was dark.

"No one at home. The lamp is still safe," said Louise with satisfaction.

She had barely spoken the words before the window sprang into a blaze of light. The Dana girls halted, astonished beyond measure.

"Why, there must be someone in our room!"

"And the door was locked!"

Beyond the curtains they could see the shadowy outline of a moving figure. Abruptly Louise changed her course toward the window. Jean followed, greatly puzzled. Someone had forced open the door of the study in their absence. Someone was now in their room. But who could it be? And why?

"It couldn't be Evelyn," she said to her sister. "She hasn't a key to our room."

"Perhaps it's Mrs. Crandall looking for us. We'll soon know."

Down beneath the window, near the place where they had seen the lurking figure on the previous night, they stood still and watched. There was certainly someone moving beyond the curtains. It was a man!

His back was turned to the window, so they could not see his face. He appeared to be bending over the table.

"Do you think," faltered Jean, "it could be —Jake Garbone?"

Louise shook her head.

"No. This man is taller and slimmer. If he would only turn around——"

At that moment the mysterious intruder straightened and moved over toward the study light. They saw that he held a sheaf of papers in his hand. He leaned over in the full glare of the beams which shone directly on his face. Then the astounded girls saw the jet-black hair, the spectacles, the little mustache—of the plumber! He was absorbed in his perusal of the papers, holding one of them up to the light for a moment, then laying it aside. Rapidly he went through the heap of documents, occasionally casting a nervous glance toward the door of the room.

Once they had recovered from their surprise, the Dana girls became indignant.

"This is too much!" declared Louise. "I don't care if he did say a good word for us to the police, I've been suspicious of that fellow all along. He's always snooping around our study, looking at the lamp——"

"We'll catch him red-handed!" snapped Jean promptly. "Let's go right up there now and ask him what he means by it."

"And then we'll report him to the Crandalls."

The mysterious plumber, in the meantime, unaware that he was being observed, went over paper after paper. He did not seem at all satisfied with what he read, for he kept shaking his head in disgust, fumbling hurriedly among the documents as if searching for one particular sheet in the sheaf.

"Come!" said Louise. "Let's hurry and catch him before he gets away!"

Quickly they ran across the campus, reached the front walk, and hurried up the stone steps.

"I can't understand it!" Jean declared. "Why should a plumber, of all people, be so interested in *our* study?"

"I don't know," replied Louise, "but if he can't explain his actions, there'll be a new workman at Starhurst tomorrow morning."

"I hope he's still there when we reach the room. Won't he be surprised!"

The Dana girls were not to fathom the mystery of the plumber just then. They were barely inside the doorway when they encountered the angular Lettie Briggs, who smiled at them in a malicious manner.

"It's about time you were showing up," she said. "I wouldn't be in your shoes for anything."

"No—they'd be miles too tight for you," said Jean, glancing at the other's inordinately large feet.

Lettie glared.

"Mrs. Crandall wants to see you in the office at once!" she said triumphantly.

CHAPTER XXII

Fay Violette Disappears

THE Dana girls received the news glumly. By their crestfallen expressions Lettie Briggs knew she had scored. However, she was not aware of the fact that the girls were less concerned with the summons to the office than they were with the knowledge that they dared not first investigate the intrusion of their study.

An immediate call from the head mistress was nothing short of a command. They knew that if they went to the study first, Lettie Briggs in the meantime would take good care to inform Mrs. Crandall that they had disregarded her orders.

"Let's hurry," said Louise, hoping that the interview would soon be over.

"You'd *better* hurry," said Lettie, as a parting thrust.

Jean tapped meekly at the office door. They heard Mrs. Crandall's voice, saying:

"Come in!"

The headmistress was seated at her desk. To their great relief, however, they saw that she did not wear the forbidding expression that was always in evidence when errant students were to be disciplined.

"This telegram arrived a few minutes ago," said Mrs. Crandall, picking up the yellow envelope from her desk. "I told Miss Briggs to let you know. And there was a telephone call, also."

Mrs. Crandall hesitated.

"Read your telegram first. Then I'll discuss the other message with you."

Louise thanked her and tore open the envelope.

A glance told her that the telegram was from Uncle Ned.

SHOCKED TO LEARN OF FRANKLIN STARR'S DISAPPEARANCE   KNOW NOTHING ABOUT IT BUT WILL DO WHAT I CAN   PLEASE PAY EVELYN STARR'S BILLS FOR THE PRESENT   WILL WRITE
UNCLE NED

Jean read the message over her sister's shoulder. The girls were naturally disappointed that their uncle was unable to throw any light on the disappearance of Franklin Starr, but were relieved to learn that they were given authority to assist Evelyn in her present difficulties.

"It's about Evelyn's brother," Louise explained, handing the message to Mrs. Crandall The headmistress read the telegram.

"A strange affair," she said thoughtfully. "Evelyn has been to me several times, asking if I had heard any news. I met Mr. Starr a few times before we purchased Starhurst. A very pleasant young man."

She nodded her head with satisfaction as she read the latter part of the message.

"If your uncle authorizes you to look after Evelyn's expenses in the meantime, I'll be glad to make any necessary advances. And now—about this telephone call."

Mrs. Crandall tapped a pencil abstractedly against the desk top.

"It was from the Penfield General Hospital," she said. "The superintendent wants to see you both."

"She wants to see us?" exclaimed Louise.

"It has something to do with a woman known as Fay Violette." Mrs. Crandall looked at the girls keenly. "Who is she?"

"She is the woman we took to the hospital yesterday," explained Jean. "We told you about our trouble with the police over the stolen car, Mrs. Crandall."

"Ah, yes, I remember. Of course, I don't like having any of my girls mixed up in this sort of affair——"

"Please, Mrs. Crandall," interrupted Jean impetuously. "If Fay Violette sent for us—she must have something important she wants to tell us."

"We had intended to ask for permission to call on her," said Louise.

"Perhaps after dinner," replied Mrs. Crandall, looking at the clock, "though I really shouldn't permit it. However, the message was urgent. I cannot allow you to go unchaperoned, so I will go with you myself."

"Will you?" exclaimed the girls, delighted.

"If you can be ready in five minutes after our meal, I'll accompany you to the hospital. Fortunately, it isn't a long walk."

Hastily the Dana girls thanked her. Then they rushed upstairs, but had little hope that the mysterious plumber would still be in the study. The door was locked, and when they unlocked it and entered the room, they found it in darkness. Louise switched on the light. The study was apparently just as they had left it.

"If we hadn't seen him through the window, we should never have guessed that anyone was here," said Jean.

"Should we tell Mrs. Crandall?"

"What do you think?"

"I'd rather wait until we have a chance to talk to the plumber personally. I'd like to know what he has to say by way of explanation. If he evades our questions or says he wasn't there, why, then we'll report him."

"That's the best plan," Jean agreed, hurriedly changing her dress.

They were soon ready, turned out the light, locked the door, and went downstairs. After dinner they joined Mrs. Crandall, and the trio set out for the hospital.

The institution was only a few blocks from Starhurst, on the outskirts of Penfield's central business section. When they reached their destination, they stated their business to the clerk at the reception desk. A moment later they were shown to an office where they confronted a stern, severe woman, who regarded them with disfavor.

"It's about this Violette woman," said the superintendent when the Dana girls had stated their business. "She has left."

"Left!" they gasped.

"Yes," snapped the superintendent, who was in no good humor.

"You mean someone came and took her away?" asked Louise.

"No," said the head of the institution, "I don't mean that."

"Then how did she get away?" asked Jean. "She seemed so ill——"

"Against all orders," the superintendent went on, "she got dressed and managed to escape from this building some time between seven o'clock and seven-thirty.

"What's more important, she left here without paying—and the hospital authorities expect you girls to pay her bill."

CHAPTER XXIII

Shadowed

THE Dana girls looked at each other in amazement as the hospital superintendent made her announcement.

"I can't see why we should pay Fay Violette's expenses," said Louise. "It's no concern of ours."

"Then whose concern is it?" demanded the superintendent. "The woman has disappeared. Her bill is unpaid. Someone will have to pay it."

"But, my goodness," objected Jean indignantly, "we did her a service. She might have died if we hadn't brought her here. We couldn't leave her where we found her."

"That's not my business. You brought that person here and you're responsible for her."

"We are *not* responsible for her," declared Louise, her eyes flashing.

"I'm asking you girls to accept the responsibility for that woman's hospital bill," retorted the superintendent arrogantly, "because she is a friend of yours."

"She is most distinctly not a friend of ours

and we refuse to do anything of the kind,''
said Jean flatly.

The superintendent, who was not the type of
woman usually found in her position, began to
bluster. Fay Violette, she declared, was a common fortune teller, a gypsy, and she hinted that
the Dana girls were closer friends of the
escaped patient than they pretended to be.

"You're responsible!" she insisted loudly.
"You brought that woman here and you are
going to pay her bill——"

"Please!" intervened Mrs. Crandall gently.
"I have heard quite enough of this nonsense."

Never before had the girls admired the headmistress as they did at that moment. She
swept the superintendent from head to toe with
a devastating glance.

"The girls did what anyone else would do,"
she said. "They found an injured woman and
they brought her to the hospital for attention.
She was admitted and placed in your care from
that moment. She seems to have been able to
walk out of here without being observed, which
doesn't say much for the solicitude she should
have been receiving. Your business is to locate
your patient and let her pay her own bill."

"But where can we locate her?"

"I imagine the sensible thing to do would be
to notify the police."

"We have already done that."

"Then why attempt to make these girls responsible for the woman's expenses? She may be found at any time.''

"She *was* staying at the Penfield House,'' Louise volunteered. "She may have gone back there.''

The superintendent noted down the name of the shabby hotel.

"The Penfield House!'' she said in an altered voice. "Well, we can make inquiries.''

"I imagine it would be to your own interest to make inquiries,'' said Mrs. Crandall acidly, "if you wish the hospital bill to be paid.''

The superintendent muttered something to the effect that she had to protect herself against impostors and spongers.

"You can do that without frightening and threatening respectable people,'' said Mrs. Crandall, as she and the girls departed.

"The idea!'' Jean fumed as they descended the steps. "A woman in her position adopting that attitude. I am very glad you came with us, Mrs. Crandall. We appreciate what you did.''

"We surely do,'' said Louise gratefully. "But she couldn't really hold us responsible for the bill, could she?''

"Of course not. But she thought she could frighten you into accepting the responsibility.''

Then Mrs. Crandall turned to the girls.

"Now,'' she said, "I want to know more about this business. You have told me fragments of it, but I'm all confused. I'd like to hear the whole story.''

''As a matter of fact,'' admitted Jean, ''we are confused, too. You see, it's about the lamp —it was stolen when we were at Oak Falls— and then Evelyn Starr's brother came along. When he saw Jake Garbone, the man who stole it, *he* disappeared—Mr. Starr, I mean—and we found his watch out at the picnic grounds, so we think Garbone must have stolen it, but it seems that Garbone wants the lamp back, for Fay Violette sold it by mistake, and she offered us ever so much money——''

''Very clear!'' interrupted Mrs. Crandall, laughing. ''Remind me tomorrow, Jean, to see that you are assigned some additional exercises in English composition. One fact *must* lead directly to the next.''

Louise smiled at her sister's discomfiture.

''It really is almost as confusing as it sounds, Mrs. Crandall. I'll begin at the beginning.''

''An excellent idea,'' commented the headmistress.

''Uncle Ned sent us a lamp from New York.''

''Very kind of him.''

''But a few minutes after we unpacked it a man entered the kitchen and stole it——''

''That,'' said Jean, ''was when Applecore broke the mirror and we had to go upstairs because we thought she was badly hurt.''

"Now Jean," cautioned Mrs. Crandall, "I think I'll understand this a great deal better if you don't try to explain it at all. Stick to the lamp, Louise."

"We followed the thief, who drove away in a car, and Jean found the car outside a second-hand shop in Oak Falls. The shop was owned by Jake Garbone, so she went inside and accused him of the theft. That was where she first saw Fay Violette. She is Garbone's sister."

As the trio made its way through the streets, Louise told the story of the mysterious chain of events that began with the theft of the lamp. Mrs. Crandall listened with growing amazement and curiosity. Louise omitted only one thing; she did not tell about the odd behavior of the plumber. This was because she felt that the man should be given an opportunity to explain his conduct if he could.

"It is all very strange," said Mrs. Crandall thoughtfully. "If the police could only lay hands on Jake Garbone, as he calls himself, I'm sure he could throw a great deal of light on the situation. He might even be able to tell what has happened to Franklin Starr."

At that moment Jean tugged at her sister's sleeve. Unnoticed by Mrs. Crandall, she pointed toward a figure who was slinking along in the shadows across the street.

Louise cast a quick glance at the man. She

was just in time to see him slip into a doorway, where he was hidden from view. She could scarcely repress an exclamation of surprise, for even in that fleeting second she had recognized the familiar, bulky figure of Jake Garbone.

"Yes," Mrs. Crandall was saying, quite oblivious of what was going on, "I'm afraid we'll remain in the dark until the police capture that man Garbone. I become nervous whenever I hear his name. And you say he was actually on the campus——"

"Watching our study window," said Louise.

"And to think that I pay wages to a watchman! A constable is supposed to patrol the grounds regularly! What sort of protection is that?"

Mrs. Crandall was indignant.

As they walked on, Louise glanced back again. The shadowy figure had emerged from the doorway and was again slinking along on the opposite pavement. He was keeping at a respectful distance, but Louise was convinced that he was following them.

Jean looked inquiringly at Mrs. Crandall. Her glance said:

"Shall we tell her?"

Louise replied by a shake of the head. Nothing would be gained, she felt sure, by telling Mrs. Crandall that at that very moment they were being shadowed by the rascally dealer. It would only make the headmistress alarmed and upset. Whatever motive Garbone might have in following them through the streets, she did not believe that he would attempt to harm them.

"Tomorrow," decided Mrs. Crandall, "I shall go to the police and insist that they keep a man posted on the campus. And I shall also," she added grimly, "reprimand them for permitting this Garbone person to remain at large. He should have been behind bars long ago."

At that moment her attention was attracted to a display of hats in a shop window. Mrs. Crandall was the last woman to be suspected of having a consuming interest in finery, but she could not resist this array.

"Now there," she said, indicating a conservative felt, "is the sort of hat I like. Smart, but not too gay, and dignified."

"I like the little red one in the corner," said Jean eagerly.

"Very well for you, my dear," replied Mrs. Crandall, "but can you fancy me in a red hat?" She laughed cheerfully. "What a picture I should make!"

The girls smiled as they thought of Mrs. Crandall wearing a red hat, particularly the frivolous little scrap of felt that had attracted Jean's attention.

There appeared to be scores of hats in the

window. This illusion was created by a number of reflectors at the rear and by mirrors on the sides. The latter were placed at such angles that they reflected also a view of a side street not actually visible from the front of the shop.

Presently, in the mirror, Louise saw the hurrying figure of a girl cast by the reflection from the street light at the corner. Her face was revealed clearly for an instant. It was the face of Evelyn Starr!

The girl scurried across the corner and vanished. Louise turned quickly and ran down to the side of the store. She could see the adjacent street from that point, but there was no one in sight. The walks were deserted.

Louise was puzzled. Had she really seen Evelyn Starr? Or was it only a trick of the mirror?

"What's the matter?" asked Jean, hurrying to her sister's side.

"Nothing," Louise answered. "I—I thought I saw someone I knew, but must have been mistaken."

They continued on their way. The Dana girls looked back to see if Jake Garbone were still trailing them, but the dealer had either hidden himself or else had decided to abandon the pursuit, for he was not in evidence.

Louise was silent as they kept on their way toward the school. She could not shake off the recollection of that strange vision of Evelyn Starr hurrying across the street corner beneath the light. Yet, what could possibly have brought the girl out at this hour of the night without permission, and in utter defiance of all the rules of Starhurst?

"I must have been mistaken," she said to herself. "My eyes were playing tricks on me."

She glanced back time and again, for the knowledge that they had been shadowed by Jake Garbone made her wary. However, the three reached the school without Louise catching any further glimpse of the man.

"I'm very glad you told me the whole story of this strange affair," said Mrs. Crandall before she parted from the Dana girls in the hall. "I shall make it my business to see that the campus is guarded more carefully in the future. Who knows but that we may learn something more about Franklin Starr before long?"

She went to her own quarters after bidding the girls good night. As they ascended the stairs, Louise told Jean about the strange vision in the store mirror.

"You must have made a mistake!" Jean insisted. "What would Evelyn be doing alone in Penfield at this time of night?"

"I'm positive I saw her," returned Louise.

"You didn't see her when you went to the corner, did you?"

"No. The street was deserted."

"Well, I don't know what to make of it," said Jean. "By every rule of Starhurst she should be in bed and asleep at this very minute."

"Let's go to her room and find out for ourselves. If she isn't in there——"

"If she isn't there, we'll have another mystery on our hands. But we had better go to our own study first. I'm worried about the lamp."

Louise unlocked the door, switching on the light as they stepped inside.

The lamp was in its usual place on the table. Nothing had been disturbed, but when Jean turned to close the door she saw a white oblong object at her feet.

Curiously she bent down and picked it up.

"A letter!" she exclaimed. "Someone must have pushed it beneath the door."

"Why, it's in Evelyn's handwriting," said Louise.

Quickly Jean tore open the envelope. The message was brief, but its contents were astonishing.

"'I am writing this letter so that you will not worry about me if I do not return to Starhurst——'"

"Not coming back to Starhurst!" exclaimed Louise, sitting down abruptly. "Then she's gone! It *was* Evelyn I saw in the mirror."

"'Tonight I received a strange message

from my brother,'" continued Jean. "'I am going to meet him. I'm afraid something very serious is the matter. If I do not come back, you will know that I have learned I cannot afford to stay on at Starhurst. I could not face the other girls unless I knew that I could pay my own way. I do wish you were here, that I might say good-bye to you, but if I don't come back, I shall write and let you know what has happened. It is good to feel, at any rate, that Franklin is alive, and that is all that matters. With best love, Evelyn.'"

There was a long silence when Jean had concluded reading this extraordinary letter.

"She has left Starhurst! Oh, if I had only told Mrs. Crandall when I saw her face in the mirror!"

"It was Evelyn, all right," agreed Jean briskly. "Let's go after her."

Louise looked doubtfully at her impetuous sister. Then she glanced at her watch.

"At this hour? It's against the rules!"

"We didn't have a chance to tell her that Uncle Ned promised to look after her bills. That might have made all the difference in the world," answered Jean, ignoring Louise's cautiousness. "Let's go to the railroad station. She was headed in that direction. Perhaps we'll find her there."

"If she went to meet her brother, she may have gone away with him on a train."

"We'll find out! Come! We can slip out onto the balcony that opens off our bedroom window, slide down the post, and go across the campus. We'll never be missed."

Louise hesitated. If they were caught, it would mean suspension or expulsion from Starhurst.

"We can't let Evelyn suffer!" urged Jean.

"I'll go!" said Louise decisively.

CHAPTER XXIV

The Jewel Case

"If we're going to slide down any balcony posts," said Jean, "I'm going to change my clothes."

"And we had better turn out the light. It throws too much of a glare, anyway. Someone might see us."

Louise switched off the study lamp. The whole school was in darkness, for the signal "lights out" had been called some time ago, and they knew that if their own window remained illuminated it might attract attention.

The girls slipped into their bedroom and changed to more serviceable clothing—dark skirts and sweaters.

"Ready?" said Jean, cautiously opening the door that led to the balcony.

"I'm ready. Go ahead."

Jean peered out. Suddenly she stiffened.

"What's the matter?" Louise whispered.

Jean retreated into the room.

"Someone is climbing up the ivy!" she said tensely.

They listened. Through the partly opened

door they heard a scuffling, followed by a slight crackling and rustling of the stout tendrils that covered the wall. The sounds seemed to come from beneath their study window.

This new development left the girls utterly bewildered for a moment. The steady upward progress of that unseen figure on the wall was infinitely menacing.

"Shall we give the alarm?" whispered Jean.

"No." Louise opened the door a little further. "We'll see who it is."

She dropped to the floor and on hands and knees crept out onto the balcony. Jean followed her example.

Through the railing they could see a dark, bulky object against the wall. A hand reached up, groped for a moment, seized a thick strand of ivy. The intruder pulled himself up closer to the window.

From below they heard a whisper.

"Be careful!" it warned.

The voice startled them. Louise looked down and saw a pallid, upturned face. Even in the gloom she recognized the figure as that of a woman. It had been a feminine voice—the voice of Fay Violette!

Their hearts beating quickly, the Dana girls watched the man on the wall. He had now reached the ledge of the open window. He dragged himself up, clinging there for a moment, resting.

"O. K.!" he growled. "I'll have it in a minute."

It was Jake Garbone!

He remained there, panting after his climb. Jean's mind worked swiftly. Once the man entered the room, their way of escape would be cut off. She tugged at her sister's sleeve.

"I'll go for help," she whispered.

Louise nodded.

Jean made scarcely a sound as she crept back into the bedroom. From there she made her way softly into the study, where she caught a glimpse of the ominous head and shoulders of the wily secondhand dealer darkly silhouetted against the unclosed window. Stealthily she opened the door to the hall and slipped out, then fled toward the stairs. Her plan was to arouse the janitor, the watchman, and the campus policeman, but she knew that if she raised an immediate general alarm, Garbone might escape in the confusion.

Meanwhile, Louise remained crouched on the balcony. From below she heard Fay Violette's anxious voice.

"Don't be all night about it!"

"Try climbing this wall yourself and see how you like it," snarled her brother in a low tone.

Slowly he began to draw himself up over the sill.

Louise retreated from the balcony and went back into the bedroom. Through the door opening into the study she could see Jake Garbone climbing over onto the window seat.

Puffing from his exertions, the man crossed the study. He went directly toward the table and reached for the lamp. Stealthily he disconnected it and picked the object up in his hands.

Louise did not know what to do. She realized she was no match for the rascally dealer, yet was aware that in another minute he would sneak away with the precious ornament, for by this time Louise was convinced that it was, for some strange reason, more valuable than they had supposed it to be. Jake Garbone would not run such tremendous risks for an ordinary lamp.

She listened, hoping for some sound from the campus—a sound that might indicate that Jean had succeeded in getting help, but everything was clothed in silence. There was not a sound save the heavy breathing of the thief in the next room, followed by a rustle and a clatter as he accidentally brushed the lamp cord off the table.

Then, through the gloom, Louise saw him run toward the window, carrying the precious object carefully in his arms. When he reached the aperture, she heard him say in a low voice:

"I have it!"

"Be quick!" replied his companion on the ground below.

Louise determined that Jake Garbone should
not escape if she could help it. Quietly she
emerged from the bedroom. Jake Garbone did
not see her as she rushed across the room, but
whirled about just as the girl reached him.
Louise grappled with all her strength, trying
to wrest the lamp from his hands.

"No, you don't!" growled the thief.

He thrust her away, again trying to reach
the window, but a second time Louise sprang
at him and grabbed the base of the lamp. Garbone wrenched it away and then, in despera-
tion, raised it aloft.

With all his force the man brought it down.
His intention was to crush Louise with the
heavy object. Had he succeeded, she would
have been knocked senseless. Luckily she realized her danger in time and sprang to one side.

The force of the blow was so great that the
beautiful article flew out of Garbone's hands,
crashing to the floor. There was a sharp ex-
plosion as the electric globe was shattered.
The top of the lamp fell off. Onto the floor
tumbled an oblong box!

Louise saw it rolling across the rug. In a
flash she realized that the little case, hidden
all the time in the base of the antique, was Jake
Garbone's real objective.

The thief saw the box, too. He lunged toward it just as Louise grabbed it. His hand
closed about her wrist in a painful grip.

"Give it to me! Give me that jewel case!"

Louise tried to wrest herself free of his grasp, but Garbone was too strong for her. The box was torn from her fingers, and in one bound the thief was at the window. In reckless haste he flung himself across the sill. By the time Louise reached the opening, he was scrambling down the ivy.

Then she heard a shrill cry of fear.

"Hurry!" shrieked Fay Violette. "There's someone coming!"

Down among the campus trees she saw a moving light, then scurrying figures. Jake Garbone uttered a cry of despair. The ivy crackled and tore away beneath his feet as he clambered hastily to reach the ground.

Louise dashed into the bedroom, then out onto the balcony. She saw Fay Violette running away, but the woman had gone no more than a few yards before a tall figure loomed up from the shadows and grabbed her by the arm. Two other men rushed out and reached the foot of the wall in time to grapple with Jake Garbone as he leaped to the ground.

The dealer struggled desperately. Fighting his way free for a moment, he dashed toward the nearest trees, but his break for liberty did not last long. One of the men overtook him in a few long strides and brought the thief crashing to the ground.

Out on the edge of the campus a police

whistle was blowing shrilly. Lights began flashing from the windows as the Starhurst students were aroused by the growing uproar. Men were shouting. Fay Violette was screaming. Garbone was bellowing angry imprecations at his captors.

Louise scrambled over the balcony rail and quickly slid down the post in a precipitate and undignified manner. She found Jake in the hands of the janitor and the campus policeman, while the Starhurst watchman was holding Fay Violette.

Jean rushed out of the shadows.

"Oh, they caught them!" she gasped. "I was afraid they would be too late."

"Caught red-handed," said the policeman grimly. "They'll be glad to see this fellow when I bring him in to the police station, Miss. We've been looking for him."

"He stole a jewel case," said Louise quickly. "Search him."

"Jewel case, eh?" The officer grabbed Garbone by the collar and shook him roughly. "Hand it over! Where is it?"

"She's lying," said Garbone defiantly. "I didn't steal anything. I haven't any jewel case."

Swiftly the officer searched him. To Louise's disappointment, the object in question was not found.

"Maybe he dropped it," suggested Jean.

The girls explored the ground beneath their window, but were unable to find the oblong box that had fallen from the study lamp.

Out on the street bordering the grounds could be heard the shrieking of a siren as a patrol wagon raced toward the school. Windows were being flung open. Girlish voices were crying:

"What's wrong? What's going on down there?"

Starhurst was awake.

"Come on!" growled the policeman, giving Garbone another shake. "Where did you hide that jewel case? Hand it over or it will be the worse for you."

"I didn't have it," the man declared sullenly. "I don't know anything about it."

"He took it from me!" insisted Louise. "It fell out of our lamp and he grabbed it. He had it when he scrambled out of the window."

"So that's why the lamp was so valuable!" said Jean in amazement.

Additional policemen came running across the grounds, and Fay Violette and her brother were soon surrounded by men in uniform. Mr. Crandall, sketchily attired in a bathrobe and a pair of tennis trousers, came bursting out of a side door, imploring everyone to tell him what had happened. There had not been so much excitement at Starhurst since the place had become a school.

"Well, Garbone," said a police lieutenant, as he confronted the prisoner, "we have you at last. You have a lot to answer for."

"You can't prove anything against me," answered the culprit.

"We can't, eh? We know that you and your sister have been crooks for years. How about Mrs. Grantland's ring? How about Mr. Grantland's car? Why, we have a list of charges a mile long against you."

"Where did you get Franklin Starr's watch?" asked Jean impulsively.

"Franklin Starr!" exclaimed Garbone. "I never heard of him."

"You had his watch. I guess you are acquainted with him."

"I don't know anything about a watch," replied the man obstinately. "And I don't know Franklin Starr."

"We'll have a few questions to ask you when you get to the police station," the lieutenant told him. "Maybe you'll feel more like talking then."

Fay Violette began to sob.

"He wanted me to help him get back the lamp," she said. "He has been trying to locate it for years. Ever since the Starr estate was sold——"

"Shut up!" yelled her brother savagely.

"It's true," she insisted. "He stole it from the Dana girls in Oak Falls when he knew their uncle had bought it. He came here tonight to get the lamp. There were jewels in it, he said."

"She's lying!" shouted Garbone. "I don't know anything about any jewels."

"Between the two of you," said the lieutenant, "I guess we'll soon know the whole story. Some of you men take a look around. He probably threw the jewel case away."

Jean turned suddenly to her sister.

"We forgot about Evelyn," she said hurriedly. "Now is our chance to hurry down to the railroad station. We'll have to tell her about that box of jewels. If it belonged to the Starr family and is recovered, it will mean the end of all her troubles."

There was so much confusion that the girls knew they could slip away unobserved.

"Let's hurry," urged Louise.

CHAPTER XXV

The Plumber's Disguise

THEIR escape from the campus was unnoticed, and as they hastened through the streets toward the station, their hearts grew lighter, for they no longer had anything to fear from Jake Garbone or his wily sister.

"I do hope the police find the jewels!" exclaimed Louise. "I can't imagine what he did with them. He must have hidden the case somewhere when he saw he couldn't escape."

"Just to think that the lamp held so much wealth!" said Jean. "Why, it would be a fortune for Evelyn and her brother." Then a sudden thought struck her. "But perhaps the case was empty."

"I'm sure it wasn't," replied Louise. "It felt very heavy, as if something was inside. Jake Garbone wouldn't have taken all that trouble and risk for nothing."

"If we can only find Evelyn in time to tell her, it may change everything."

"I have been wondering," said Louise as they hurried on, "why that plumber was so interested in the lamp."

"Perhaps he knew about the jewels, too, and meant to steal it."

Louise smiled.

"I have a hunch about that plumber. When he was talking to us in the police station, I had a feeling that his voice was familiar."

"What's your hunch?" asked Jean curiously. But Louise would not enlighten her sister.

"I may be wrong," she said. "However, I'm sure I know now why the plumber acted so strangely."

"Do you think he was a detective?"

"Not exactly."

They came in sight of the station. In a few minutes the girls were hurrying up the platform.

"We've lost so much time," said Jean, "that Evelyn may be miles away by now. In fact, she may not have been coming here at all."

Just then, through an open window of the waiting room, Louise caught sight of two figures.

"Look!" she whispered.

Evelyn Starr and the mysterious "plumber" were deep in conversation. As the Dana girls watched, they saw that Evelyn was in tears. The man took her in his arms and kissed her. Then Jean realized the truth.

"Oh, it's Franklin Starr himself!"

"Ssh!" whispered Louise. "My hunch was right. Listen!"

"I worried so much about you, Franklin," sobbed the sad girl. "I thought you were dead."

"Occasionally I have wished I were," he said with emotion. "My head ached so severely at times after my experience when the Dana girls rescued me, I was nearly crazy. Then," the poor fellow continued, "our losses have been dreadful. I couldn't sleep or eat, thinking about them. My only thought was to search the old homestead, Evelyn, and see if I could find something of value hidden there.

"I was afraid to let you know my secret. It would have spoiled all my plans if anyone were to know. I dyed my hair, grew this mustache, donned spectacles, then got that job, so that I could come and go in Starhurst without being suspected."

"But you took such risks," said Evelyn. "Suppose Mrs. Crandall had found out——"

"But I was desperate, Evelyn," the "plumber" continued. "I couldn't bear the thought of facing poverty—not for my sake, but for yours. I wanted you to finish your education, and have always been certain that there is wealth belonging to us hidden somewhere in Starhurst. I determined to go and search for it, but I did not wish to be laughed at if nothing came of it, so I wore the disguise."

"You didn't find *anything?*"

Franklin Starr shook his head sadly.

"We're beaten, I'm afraid. I thought I had stumbled on something of value when I found a secret panel in the Dana girls' study. You remember that was the old library when we owned Starhurst."

"Wasn't there anything hidden behind the panel?" asked Evelyn eagerly.

"Some old papers. I was sure they were valuable, but on looking them over I found that they weren't. Nothing but worthless old sheets, so I decided to give up the search. That's why I sent you the message to meet me here. I wanted to tell you the truth. It's no use trying to mince words—we haven't any money, so we'll just have to make the best of it."

The Dana girls strained their ears to catch Evelyn's softly spoken reply.

"I don't care, Franklin," replied Evelyn. "As long as I know you're safe and well, nothing else counts. We'll go away together and I'll keep house for you. It doesn't matter about my education. I don't care if we're poor."

"But I *know*, Evelyn—I just *know* that our father left us a fortune hidden somewhere. When I found those papers, I was sure I had stumbled on the secret. I thought they were bonds or stock certificates."

The Dana girls waited no longer. Louise thrust open the door of the waiting room and they hurried inside. Evelyn and her brother

looked disturbed and embarrassed as the girls
approached them.

"Hello, Mr. Starr," said Louise, smiling.

"Then you knew all the time?" gasped
Evelyn.

"No, I didn't. But I had a hunch."

"We read your note, Evelyn," said Jean
breathlessly. "That's why we came here. But
so many things have happened——"

"We want you to come back to Starhurst.
You mustn't run away like this."

"I'm afraid," said Franklin Starr seriously,
"that Evelyn can't go back. You seem to have
penetrated my disguise, so I may as well explain why I was posing as a plumber——"

"We know," interrupted Louise. "We realize you were searching for your fortune, and
you did not wish Evelyn to learn about it. But
you might not have been looking in the right
place," she concluded wisely.

Franklin Starr leaned forward.

"The lamp?" he asked in a tense voice.

Louise nodded.

"Did you know that there was a jewel case
hidden in the lamp?"

"The Starr jewels!" exclaimed Franklin
Starr. "They have been missing ever since my
father died. I thought they had been sold.
Surely you haven't found them?"

His face was alight with hope. That strained
expression as of a deranged mind had left his

countenance completely. The Dana girls noticed it at once. Louise wished heartily that she had not mentioned the precious stones, for she divined what disappointment would mean to this earnest fellow.

"I'm sorry," she said gently, "but tonight a man named Jake Garbone——"

A shadow crossed Franklin Starr's hopeful visage.

"Garbone," he said bitterly. "The man who stole our family heirlooms. My watch was among them. It was given to me by my father."

"He came to the school tonight and tried to steal the lamp. He must have suspected that the jewel case was inside."

"He escaped!" said Starr, his face blanched.

Louise then told the story of Jake Garbone's disastrous attempt at burglary. She related how she had tried to wrest the lamp from the man's hands, how he had endeavored to strike her, how the jewel case had rolled out onto the floor, and how Garbone had snatched it up and fled.

"He was caught by the police," she concluded, "but although they searched him, they could find no trace of the box. He must have hidden it somewhere. Yet there is a good chance that it may be found. That's why you mustn't think of taking Evelyn away from Starhurst."

"Oh, if the jewels could only be brought to

light!" said Evelyn in excitement. "All our troubles would then be over."

"The Starr jewels," said her brother quietly, "are worth between fifty and sixty thousand dollars. They represent a comfortable fortune. If Garbone didn't have them in his pockets, he must have managed to hide them somewhere near by."

"The police may have found them by this time," Jean pointed out. "Why don't you come back with us? If there is a chance of recovering that fortune, you mustn't go away."

"Yes," said Franklin Starr quickly and firmly, "we'll go back."

Evelyn's face had brightened at the prospect of recovering the lost property.

"It's too much to hope for " she said. "I daren't let myself think there is a chance of finding the jewels. The box might have been empty."

So, wavering between brightest hope and darkest despair, Franklin Starr and Evelyn went back to Starhurst with the Dana girls. On their way through the streets they saw a patrol wagon go speeding by. Jake Garbone and Fay Violette, in the hands of the law, would soon answer for their many crimes.

Lights were ablaze throughout the school as they passed through the gate and went up the walk, but the Dana girls' study window was quite dark.

"Poor old lamp!" said Jean softly. "I hope we can get it repaired."

Just then they encountered the school watchman. When he recognized the girls he touched his hat.

"They've taken 'em away to clap 'em behind bars," he announced.

"Did the police find the jewels?" asked Jean eagerly.

"Jewels?" returned the man blankly. "What jewels? No, they didn't find any that I heard of. But they found a box."

"The jewel case. Where was it?"

"Hidden right at the bottom of the ivy," the watchman told them. "That villain must have put it there when he saw he was going to be caught."

"What was in it?" asked Franklin Starr.

"Nothin', sir. Nothin' at all. The box was empty."

Franklin Starr groaned.

"Our last hope," he said.

The watchman looked at him curiously. Then he turned to the Dana girls.

"The janitor went up to your study to fix your lamp," he said. "It wasn't badly broken. Just needed a new bulb, that's all, once it was fitted together again. Ah—it's fixed now."

As he spoke, the study window shone with a strong and brilliant light. It was a much more powerful gleam than the lamp had cast before and its rays streamed onto the ivy beneath the window.

"Didn't have no more of the ordinary size bulbs," the watchman explained, "so he had to use large ones. Myself, I like a good strong light."

He wandered off down the walk.

Crushed with disappointment, Franklin Starr and his sister accompanied the Dana girls toward the front steps.

"The box was empty," said Franklin, his voice trembling. "I had hoped—oh, well, no use crying over what might have been. We're not to be wealthy again after all, Evelyn."

"It doesn't matter," she replied bravely.

At that moment, however, there arose a sudden and simultaneous shout from the Dana girls. Their faces were radiant with incredulous delight and surprise as they stood pointing at the trailing mass of vines just beneath their rooms.

"The jewels!" shrieked Jean.

The strong light of the study lamp reflected gleams of crimson, and green, and fiery white. Precious stones shone and sparkled in dazzling splendor among the vines, catching up the rays of light and transforming them into radiant color. Pearls, diamonds, emeralds, and rubies, a veritable fortune, dangled from the ivy where they had caught when the jewel box had fallen from Jake Garbone's hand.

The study lamp shone clearly and steadily. It had cast its glowing rays into the darkness of despair and had revealed a future of happiness and comfort for Evelyn Starr and her brother.

Ecstatic with happiness, they greeted Mrs. Crandall, who was waiting, and then they all rushed into the school and hastened to the study. There Louise leaned out of the window and recovered the jewels from among the vines. Evelyn was tremulous with joy. She could scarcely speak, but relief and delight shone from her eyes.

"The jewel box was *not* empty," said Louise proudly, as she thrust the precious stones into Franklin Starr's hand.

"I—I don't know what to say," he stammered, overcome by the realization that the gloomy spectre of poverty need no longer trouble them. "If you only knew what it means to us—to Evelyn——"

"We know," said Jean quietly. "And we are as happy as you are."

"How can we ever thank you and Louise?" asked Evelyn, her voice breaking. "If you hadn't recovered the lamp—if you hadn't saved it from Jake Garbone, we should never have obtained our fortune. I can hardly believe it's really true."

Her feelings were too deep to express in words. She burst into tears, but they were tears of happiness. Evelyn knew that now she could not only remain at Starhurst, but that she would no longer need to worry about the future. Her brother could take his rightful place in the world, unhampered by debts.

The Crandalls were eager to hear all about the details, especially Professor Crandall, who had been completely unaware of the strange doings about Starhurst, so deeply engrossed was he in his writings on Grecian history.

"Great girls!" he praised. "Great girls! You have solved several interesting mysteries, and I give you much credit."

The professor was to do so very soon again, for the sisters were to be called upon to help solve "The Secret at Lone Tree Cottage," a story concerning one of their instructors.

"Uncle Ned will be pleased to hear our story about the wonderful secret his gift held, Louise," laughed Jean gaily.

Her sister smiled sweetly.

"Yes," she said, "it has all worked out for the best, and Jean, I'll never forget how those precious jewels looked by the light of the study lamp."